The PRIZE WINNERS of PIEDMONT PLACE

Escape from Funland

Also by Bill Doyle

The Prizewinners of Piedmont Place

★　★　★

Attack of the Shark-Headed Zombie
Stampede of the Supermarket Slugs
Invasion of the Junkyard Hog

The PRIZE WINNERS of PIEDMONT PLACE

Escape from Funland

Book 2

by **Bill Doyle**

illustrated by **Colin Jack**

Random House 🏠 New York

Text copyright © 2017 by Bill Doyle
Jacket art and interior illustrations copyright © 2017 by Colin Jack

All rights reserved. Published in the United States by
Random House Children's Books, a division of
Penguin Random House LLC, New York.

Random House and the colophon are registered trademarks of
Penguin Random House LLC.

Visit us on the Web! randomhousekids.com

Educators and librarians, for a variety of teaching tools,
visit us at RHTeachersLibrarians.com

Library of Congress Cataloging-in-Publication Data
Names: Doyle, Bill H., author. | Jack, Colin, illustrator.
Title: Escape from funland / by Bill Doyle ; illustrated by Colin Jack.
Description: First edition. | New York : Random House, [2017] |
Series: The Prizewinners of Piedmont Place ; book 2 |
Summary: The Talaska family enters a contest to win a home makeover.
Identifiers: LCCN 2015038762 | ISBN 978-0-553-52181-8 (hardcover) |
ISBN 978-0-553-52183-2 (ebook)
Subjects: | CYAC: Family life—Fiction. | Contests—Fiction. | Dwellings—
Remodeling—Fiction. | Humorous stories.
Classification: LCC PZ7.D7725 Ex 2017 | DDC [Fic]—dc23

Printed in the United States of America
10 9 8 7 6 5 4 3 2 1
First Edition

Is your house falling down?
Time to call in the Head Clown!

FUNLAND FUN HOUSE MAKEOVER CONTEST

Want a slide to the outside, a bumper-car kitchen–
or maybe a trampoline bed?
Our clown squad will turn your old
home into a new fun house!

PLUS: Your town will WIN $10,000!

The contest will run each month until
we have a winning family.... ENTER NOW!

FUNLAND AMUSEMENT PARK
We can't wait to make you LIKE us!

When water dribbled onto the T. rex's head, Cal Talaska wondered if he had gone too far.

The eleven-year-old was balanced on a wobbly chair in his basement on Piedmont Place. He had just peeled back duct tape from a cracked pipe that ran along the ceiling.

Plip! Plop! Plop!

Warm water dripped from the pipe onto the card table below, where two dinosaurs were locked in battle. Cal had molded green clay into a T. rex fighting a brontosaurus and posed them next to a pond made out of tinfoil. The water splashed off the dinos and filled the foil pond—just as he had planned.

"What are you up to, Cal?" It was a girl's voice.

Startled, Cal almost tumbled off the chair onto the

nearby washing machine. He turned to find his nine-year-old sister peering up at him suspiciously. Cal had been so wrapped up in his plan that he hadn't heard Imo come downstairs.

"You're the one sneaking around," Cal said. "I'm not up to anything." But of course he was up to something, something very important. He just wasn't ready to say what yet. To distract Imo, he pointed to nothing behind her. "Holy Aristotle, what's *that*?"

"Ugh, Cal, nice try," Imo said, keeping her eyes fixed on the clay models and the foil. "Hey, that looks like the dinosaur waterfall at the Funland Fun House."

That's right! Cal thought proudly. He *had* created a mini version of the famous fun house. But he wanted their mom to see it first. Cal had an idea to sell to his family. He thought the best way to convince them was to do it one person at a time—starting with his mom. And right now his sister was messing up that plan.

"I'm not *sneaking around,* by the way," Imo added. "Bug is looking for his seesaw. So I tiptoed down here to make sure he can't find it."

Cal and Imo's parents had hidden their four-year-old brother's plastic seesaw in the basement. Bug and the family dog had started using it as a catapult in their Bug & Butler Spectacular Stunts.

"Better question: What are you doing down here, Cal?" Imo asked as she grabbed a stack of old sweaters from a plastic bin. She heaped them on top of the seesaw, which had been tucked into the back of a shelf. Soon it was buried from view.

"Okay, I'll tell you part of it," Cal said. "I'm just waiting for Mom so I can ask her something . . . *alone.*"

Ignoring Cal's hint for her to leave, Imo squinted past him at the dial on the washing machine. "Well, she'll be down any second," she said. "Orca is almost done."

Cal knew she was right. Mrs. T. would hustle downstairs to switch the clothes to the dryer the second Orca's timer buzzed.

The Talaskas had named the washing machine Orca after a killer whale. If clothes sat inside for even a minute after the washing machine was done, Orca would pop back to life and start spinning crazily. The entire machine would lift off the concrete floor as it rocked back and forth. By the time it stopped, clothes came out looking like they'd been chewed up and spit out by a whale.

Usually on Sunday afternoons, their dad took charge of the laundry. But right now Mr. T. was upstairs in the shower. Even two floors away, Cal could hear him singing in his deep, off-key voice, *"Oh, you bewitching bonanza of bronzed bread!"*

Cal imagined the shower water whooshing into the drain, rushing through the long pipe that ran down to the basement, and finally running into the dripping pipe over his head.

"I put that tape around that leak for a reason, Cal," Imo said. "I insist you get off that chair and tell me what you're doing."

Insist? Cal wanted to laugh. He was saved from answering by tiny footsteps bounding down the stairs. Their little brother flew around the corner at full speed. Bug obviously had one thing on his mind: the seesaw. Cal tried to distract him.

"Holy Aristotle, what's *that*?" Cal pointed away from the shelf. But Bug ignored him, too.

Like a hound dog on a scent, Bug went straight for the shelf where Imo had been stuffing sweaters.

"Wasees!" Bug shouted.

Cal figured that must be Bug's word for *seesaw*. For a few weeks Bug had only barked. Now he was talking again. Well, sort of. He made up words that only Butler, the family dog, seemed to understand. Imo called it the boy/dog language, or Bog for short, and she had even started recording it.

Tossing aside the sweaters, Bug dragged the see-saw from the shelf and put it on the floor between Cal and Orca. Bug planted himself on one end, and then he gazed up at Imo with round, pleading eyes as if to say, *Please, please, please seesaw with me.*

Bug was famous for his wild tantrums when he didn't get his way—and clearly, Imo didn't want to risk it. "All right, all right," she said, and sat on the other end of the seesaw. "But no catapulting!"

This was too much for Cal. Why didn't they just go already? He wanted their mom's full attention when she came down.

"Come on, guys!" he said as Imo and Bug seesawed away. "Can't you do that anywhere else?"

Imo opened her mouth, and this was what came out: "*Buzz!*" She clapped a hand over her lips.

Actually, it was Orca. The washing machine was done . . . for now. Imo laughed. "I couldn't have said it better myself."

Just as Cal expected, the wooden steps creaked as

their mom headed downstairs from the kitchen. She was taking her time on the rickety staircase.

Cal had only seconds to put the finishing touches on his plan. He'd just have to deal with Imo and Bug sticking around. He reached up and pulled back the tape around the pipe a little more for the full dinosaur water-fall effect—*SPLITH!*

Uh-oh.

The tape tore away part of the rusty metal around the leak. Now the hole in the pipe was much bigger. The dribble of water was a steady stream, like something out of a garden hose, spraying the dinosaurs and overflowing the foil pond. The water ran onto the table and the floor.

"Cal!" Imo cried.

"It's all good," Cal said. But it wasn't. "I just have to put the tape back." On his tiptoes, Cal leaned over the table to cover the hole. He blocked the leak by holding the tape in place. Then he tried to stand up straight again. He couldn't. He was tilted too far forward, like the slope of a low hill. His toes balanced on the chair, and his hand pressed against the pipe. He could feel the pipe cracking under his fingers.

"Don't move!" Imo commanded. From her seat on the seesaw, she reached for Cal and grabbed the back of his belt. "Uh!" she grunted, straining. She kept him from falling completely against the pipe and breaking it—but just barely.

That was when their mom turned the corner from the bottom of the stairs. Her eyes went wide. "What the garbanzo is going on?" she demanded.

"Help, Mom!" Imo gasped. About to get dragged off the seesaw, Imo latched her free hand onto Mrs. T.'s belt. Both of Imo's arms were stretched out to her sides, one toward her brother and the other toward her mother.

"Garbanzo!" Mrs. T. repeated as Imo yanked her forward. To keep from falling over, her hands shot out behind her and grasped the sides of Orca.

Now Mrs. T. was the anchor holding Imo and Cal in place. If their mom let go, Imo would tilt to the side, Cal would fall into the pipe, the pipe would break, and water would flood the basement.

"Doog ton," Bug chirped, and started to get off the seesaw.

"No!" Imo said. As Bug moved, Imo's side of the seesaw sank a few inches. Her arms stretched even more, and she nearly let go of Cal. "Sit down, Bug!"

Bug threw himself back on the seesaw. And Imo's end rose again. Even his small body was enough to balance things out.

"Can you pull Cal so he can stand up, Imo?" Mrs. T. asked through gritted teeth.

Cal felt a tug on his belt as Imo strained to bring him back on his feet. "I can't from this angle!" she said.

Mrs. T. nodded, clearly trying not to panic. "Okay, that water is coming from your dad's shower," she said. "He'll stop soon and so will the water going through the pipe. We just have to hold on till then."

"Um," Cal mumbled, "it might be a little longer than *soon*."

Mrs. T. knew that tone of voice. "What did you do, Cal?"

"Nothing," Cal said. "Well, I might've challenged Dad to write a song about toast." He paused and then added, "Using every letter of the alphabet."

Imo groaned. "Why would you do that? Did you want this to happen?"

"Not this exactly!" Cal answered. "I told him I'd take five-second showers for a month to make up for the wasted water."

"You were trying to divide and conquer, weren't you?" Mrs. T. said. "Get me alone so I'd say yes to a new idea you have? And then you'd tell your dad I said yes and so should he, right? That way you could play us off each other."

"Wow." Even dangling in this wobbly spot, Cal was impressed. His mom had guessed exactly what he was doing. "I do have an idea for our next contest," he admitted. "I wanted you to see how the house needs fixing up *and* how much fun Funland can—"

"Shh for a minute!" Imo said. "I'm trying to hear where Dad is in the alphabet."

Over the gurgling sounds from Orca, they could

hear Mr. T.'s voice from two stories away. *"Great gorgeous grilled grains!"* he sang.

"Holy Aristotle," Cal moaned. "He's only on *G*."

"If he spends twenty seconds on each letter of the alphabet"—Imo did the math in her head—"he won't be finished in the shower for another six minutes and twenty seconds."

"I won't make it that long," Cal said. His toes were quivering. "I'm going to fall through this pipe at any second." His mind raced and landed on an idea. "Bug, call Butler!"

Bug nodded and yelled something in Bog that sounded like "Emoc!" Before he had even finished, Butler barked back "Rabbo!" from somewhere outside.

After an instant, Butler bounded down the stairs and burst into the basement and went straight to Bug. The dog's tail twirled, and even though he was the size of a baby hippo, his feet barely touched the ground as he spun happily. Butler and Bug always had a spectacular reunion, even if they had been apart for only thirty seconds.

Circling the seesaw and knocking into the shelves, Butler tried to get closer to Bug.

"Ysae!" Bug said, and Butler sat still. His brown-flecked eyes went from one Talaska to the next. The dog's long tongue popped out, and he cocked his head to the left. His look said, *I don't get what's happening, but I totally want to be part of it!*

That's perfect, Cal thought, *because I've got a job for you.* "Bug," he said, "tell Butler to go upstairs and get Dad!"

With another nod, Bug tapped Butler's nose and said something in gibberish that sounded like "Dad teg og!"

"Rabbo!" Butler barked. His paws scraped on the concrete, and he took off up the stairs. They heard him dash through the kitchen over their heads—hitting the squeaky board that always sounded like someone saying "Hi!"—through the living room, and then up to the second floor. There was a pause, and Cal pictured Butler opening the bathroom door with his front paws.

Seconds later, they heard Mr. T. yell, "Whoa!" Cal imagined Butler jumping into the small shower with his dad and spinning with excitement.

"Cold! Cold! Cold!" Mr. T. shouted. Butler's swinging tail must have knocked the shower handle and turned the water to freezing. Even leaning at this weird angle, Cal couldn't help it. He started laughing.

"Don't!" Imo warned. "You're bouncing!" But then she was laughing, too. Her stretched arms waggled up and down. "What's happening upstairs?" she asked.

Mrs. T. chuckled. "The Butler did it!" Bug jiggled

happily on the seesaw, and the whole chain of Talaskas nearly collapsed. It was an old family joke to answer any question that might get someone in trouble with "The Butler did it!" Mrs. T. said she got the idea from reading whodunits where the butler always wound up being the crook. And the joke never failed to get laughs.

Dripping wet, Mr. T. clambered down the creaking

stairs in his slippers and bath-robe to find the rest of the family linked together and giggling. His fogged-up glasses were on a slant.

"What's going on with you guys?" he said. "Why'd Butler give me that icy surprise?" Whenever Mr. T. got nervous or excited, he couldn't help but rhyme. Butler galloped down the stairs, shook off the shower water, and squirmed past Mr. T. to get near Bug.

"Uh, a little help, Dad," Cal said. The leak had stopped, but he was still afraid to move. He didn't want to break the pipe.

"Can someone please explain how you wound up in this weird chain?" Mr. T. asked, grabbing Cal by the waist. Cal's dad was strong and easily lifted him off the chair and put him on the floor. Imo let go of Cal and Mrs. T., and Mrs. T. let go of Orca. Bug popped off the seesaw, and he and Butler finally had their dramatic reunion. They squirmed and squealed together as everyone talked at once.

Mrs. T.: "It's this pipe! We'll have to stop using that shower!"

Imo: "Those stairs might collapse. I can't keep up with repairs—"

Bug: "Nuf!"

Butler: "Rabbo!"

Cal gave up on telling his idea to one person at a time. He decided he might as well announce his big plan now.

"Prizewinners of Piedmont Place, I give you our next great adventure!" Cal shouted, pointing to the clay dinosaurs that had been smooshed by the leak. "It's the Funland Fun House Makeover Contest!"

Just then the washing machine exploded.

Like water spurting from a whale's blowhole, a geyser of suds and clothes shot up out of Orca and hit the ceiling with a loud *splop!*

There was a fraction of a second when the clothes stuck to the ceiling and the whole family glared at Cal.

"Whoa!" Cal said. "I did *not* plan that!"

Then the clothes fell like wet, soapy missiles. *Splat!* A tangle of soggy knee socks splashed onto Imo's shoulder. *Splish!* Plaid pants squished onto Cal's face. "Shmoly Sharistotle!" he said, before yanking away the wet fabric.

A pair of boxer shorts plopped onto Mr. T.'s head as he leaned over to pull Orca's plug out of the wall socket.

"Everyone out!" Mrs. T. shouted. She threw open the door that led directly to the backyard. Fresh air poured in and the Talaskas poured out, peeling drenched dish towels, sweatshirts, and pants off their bodies.

Even without power, Orca shot one last spray of water at them before finally going still with a shudder. In the backyard, Cal silently thanked the washing machine. Without its nutty behavior, Cal's parents might have focused on him messing around with the leaky pipe. As it was, they were more worried about all the wet clothes.

Mrs. T. went into action mode. "We'd better not use the dryer," she said. "It might not be safe."

A few storage boxes had been splashed by Orca. The Talaskas dragged the boxes and the wet clothes outside. They covered the patio furniture with socks so they'd dry in the sun. Butler galloped around the yard, shaking a pair of Imo's overalls in his mouth.

"Butler, knock it—!" Imo started, then stopped. "Actually, thanks! That gives me an idea. Be right back!"

Imo rushed into the fort shaped like a bank from the Old West that sat in the far corner of the yard. That was Imo's workshop, where she dreamed up inventions.

A minute later, Imo emerged holding something bulky in both arms. She had clamped plastic antlers to the front of a remote-control car. It looked like an odd robotic deer.

What's she up to now? Cal wondered to himself.

The whole family watched, mystified, as Imo put the horned car down on the grass and trotted over to the pile of wet clothes. She plucked out the purple shirts that the Talaskas had made for the first contest they had entered and hung them on the horns. Finally, she flicked the car's on switch, and the vehicle took off across the lawn. Imo had taped the remote-control stick to one side, so the car drove in big circles around the yard. The shirts flapped in the breeze.

"Instant dryer!" Imo crowed.

As the car whizzed by Butler, he jumped back and growled. "Rabbo!"

"In my opinion, you're just jealous, Butler!" Imo laughed. Cal's sister was a year and a half younger than he was, but she could have much stronger opinions about things. In fact, that was why barely anyone called her by her real name, Jessie. Most people used her nickname, Imo—which was short for *in my opinion*. But that didn't mean Cal always agreed with her opinions. Like now.

"You think Butler's jealous of a battery-powered moose?" Cal scoffed as he put down a box of papers that he had just lugged out of the basement. "No way."

"Whatever, Cal." Imo rolled her eyes. "What is all that junk?" She crouched and started rooting through the box. Mr. and Mrs. T. came over to take a look as well.

"What's this doing in here?" Mrs. T. carefully pushed aside one of the soggy sheets of paper and reached for a shiny object. It was the family bell.

This wasn't the giant gold gong the family had won in the Great Grab Contest, when they had raced through a store for twenty minutes, grabbing everything they wanted. They had sold that gong and its mallet to pay bills and help Bug's babysitter pay for college.

The new, simple copper bell was the size of a small apple and had a plain handle like a toothbrush. It was a gift from Grandma Gigi. Cal's grandmother rhymed every once in a while, but she was the most serious of anyone in the family. She didn't put up with any nonsense. She had sent the bell with a card that had only one word on it: *Proud.*

"Why's this in here?" Mrs. T. repeated, holding out the bell.

Cal took it and thought, *Okay, it's now or never.*

He gave the bell a sharp ring. Like Gigi, the sound was quick and to the point. *Ting!* The Talaskas had a rule that when the bell was rung, everyone had to stop and listen. Cal put the bell down as his family gathered closer around him. They took seats on the grass, and Bug snuggled up against Butler's side as if he were a furry beanbag chair.

Once everyone was settled, Mr. T. said, "Okay, Cal, what's up?"

Cal cleared his throat. "Mom and Dad, remember when you told me that I'm the quarterback of the contests we pick? Well, the dictionary defines *quarterback* as—"

"Uh, honey?" Mrs. T. rolled her hand in a hurry-it-along motion. "Your audience is wearing wet underwear here."

Good point, Cal thought. "Now that we're the Prizewinners of Piedmont Place," he said, picking up speed,

"I've been looking at other contests for us to enter. All this stuff is part of my Contest Incubator filled with possible ideas." Cal pushed the box toward his audience.

His family leaned forward to take out soggy pamphlets or printouts. Chuckling, Imo read the paper in her hand. "'To win this contest, you have to eat twelve raw rutabagas in ten minutes'!"

"How about this one?" Mrs. T. shook a damp flyer. "'You need to run a triple marathon in a single day.'"

"Enob!" Bug chirped, waving a waterlogged pamphlet with a dog bone on the front. Butler's tail thumped happily on the grass.

"No, I've got the best," Mr. T. said with a laugh, as if he'd found the biggest joke of them all. "The Funland Fun House Makeover Contest!"

"Actually . . . ," Cal said.

Mr. T. held the flyer out for Mrs. T. to see. She laughed, too, as she read, "'Our clown squad will turn your old home into a new fun house!'"

"Hilarious!" Imo said.

When Cal didn't join in the laughter, Mrs. T. suddenly realized something. "Wait," she said. "That's why you wanted us to see the dripping pipe?"

"And hear the creaking stairs and watch Orca spin

out of control," Cal added. "It's the perfect contest for us! The clowns will come and fix everything up!"

Mr. T. slanted his glasses as if that would give him a better look at the flyer. "It's sponsored by Funland . . . as in Funland Amusement Park?" Then he sang the slogan, *"We can't wait to make you LIKE us!"*

Imo tugged her ear, and Cal took this as a good sign. It meant she was thinking seriously about something. "Hasn't Funland been closed for a couple of years while they make changes to the park?"

"Actually, they shut the gates thirty-six months and three days ago," Mrs. T. said. As always, Cal was amazed by the facts his mom knew. He wasn't sure how she kept everything stored so neatly in her brain.

Mr. T. was still scanning the flyer. "Each month Funland has the same two-stage makeover contest. Lots of families make it past Stage One, but no one has ever won Stage Two."

"That's why it's so great!" Cal said. "People are scared to try anymore, and that makes our odds of winning even better!"

"It sounds too hard," Mrs. T. said. "We need a sure thing. How about one that's easier?" She pulled out her phone and ran a search. "Here's a contest to build a better Popsicle stick. And one to see who can stand in place the longest."

Before Cal could say anything, Imo beat him to the punch. "In my opinion, those contests don't sound like *us*."

Mrs. T. nodded. "You're right. And now that I look, the dates are all wrong. We need to win a new contest . . . now. Or at least in the next thirty days."

"Why thirty days?" Cal asked.

For a second Mr. and Mrs. T. shared a look as if trying to decide how to answer. Finally, Mrs. T. sighed. "Take a gander at the house, you guys."

Imo, Cal, Bug, and Butler did just that. As always, Cal liked the way their house resembled a tilting ship that had just crashed onto shore. He liked how the slumped roof trapped baseballs he accidentally hit up there with his friends. He liked how the gutters got clogged with leaves from the giant trees that drooped over the house. The leaves made a soupy goop that smelled the best on warm fall days. He liked the cracks in the patio that made the shape of a smiling face. He liked how the crooked chimney formed an arrow pointing the family toward the future.

"It might not be perfect," Cal said. "But it's close."

Mrs. T. followed his gaze, making sure they were looking at the same thing. "Cal, the house is a wreck."

"Shh, please," Cal said, as if the house could hear them.

Mr. T. let out a long breath. "There's no easy way to say this," he said. "We're going to sell the house."

"What?" Cal and Imo cried at the same time, and Bug squealed, "Tahw!" They had all leapt to their feet without Cal even realizing it.

This can't be happening, he thought. "I'm sorry about the leaking pipe! Imo can fix it!" he said. "We can't move!"

Cal's whole plan was backfiring. He had wanted his family to see a few of the house's minor flaws so that they would enter the Funland makeover contest, not so that they would move. What would the Talaskas do without the best house ever? Or the kooky Rivales as neighbors? Or the quick walk to the Donegan Diner?

"Honey, this has nothing to do with today," Mrs. T. soothed, guessing what he was thinking. "This isn't easy for any of us. Your dad has lived in this house all his life. And Grandma Gigi before him."

"There's too much out of whack," Mr. T. said. "Like the plumbing and the roof and the cracked foundation."

"Imo can take care of it!" Cal insisted. But as he said it, he knew that not even Imo could fix all that stuff.

"What's going to happen to the house?" Imo asked, then pointed past the circling toy car to the fort. "And what about my workshop?"

Dropping her gaze, Mrs. T. shrugged sadly. "The next owners might just knock everything down and start over."

Imo gasped and Cal was struck speechless, but Bug chirped, "Kcis!"

"Bug's right," Imo said, guessing what he meant. "The house is just kind of sick. We can make it better."

Mrs. T. looked to Mr. T. for help. "Listen, guys," he said. "We made a little money selling things from the Great Grab Contest, but this house needs a lot more. Now that I'm not working at Mr. Wylot's factory . . ."

"Which is a good thing!" Mrs. T. squeezed his arm. "It just means we're making less money each month. We put an ad for the house online to see if we might get a bite."

She held out her phone so Cal and Imo could see the ad. Mrs. T. had posted a few small pictures of the house, including one of the Talaskas grinning in the backyard last summer. Cal flicked his finger on the screen to scroll down. Under the photos, people from all over the country had left comments. Most of them were pretty awful:

HA! For sale? You would have to PAY ME to live there!

What's wrong with that stupid staircase?
And that ridiculous kitchen!

Is that a house or the town junkyard?
Those patio cracks are UGLY!

Why is that little girl wearing those
dumb clips in her hair?

Cal tried to cover up the screen before Imo could read that last comment. Mrs. T. must have seen it, too, because she pulled the phone away.

"We got a ton of mean comments from people," Mrs. T. said. "But in two hours someone offered to buy the house. We've got thirty days to accept the deal. If we don't figure out some other way to fix things up, we'll have to sell the house and move."

Cal had a feeling he knew who "someone" was. He was sure it was the Wylots. They owned more than half the town and seemed to want nothing more than to make the Talaskas' lives miserable.

"No, it's *not* the Wylots, Cal," Mrs. T. said, again

guessing what he was thinking. "They're the Bentons, and they're from Chicago. They have two kids and a cat. And they have a reality show online about fixing up old houses. Mr. Benton said this place would be their biggest challenge yet."

Imo tapped her chin. "I don't remember them visiting. Have they even seen the house?"

"Not in person," Mrs. T. said. "We sent them pictures and we invited them to spend the night anytime they want."

Groaning, Cal spun away from them. He couldn't believe this was happening. "How can we be the Prizewinners of Piedmont Place if we don't live on Piedmont Place anymore?"

Mr. T. gently turned him back around by his shoulders. "Cal, the six of us are always going to be together," Mr. T. said. "It's your mom's and my job to put a roof over your heads. You don't have to worry about that."

"I know, Dad, thanks," Cal said. "But I want the roof to be this one."

"Me too," agreed Imo, digging her heels into the ground, and Bug chimed in, "Oot, em!"

Putting his hands in his pockets as if unsure what

to do with them, Mr. T said, "Well I don't know what to suggest. Maybe we could try this Funland contest?"

Mrs. T. pushed the hair away from her face. "I don't want to get anyone's hopes up too much. . . ."

Now was Cal's chance to nudge everyone more toward his plan. He could see that his parents were on the brink. Persuading people was one of his main talents, and he knew just the thing to get them to say yes.

"The makeover contest isn't just about us," he said quickly. "The winners' town gets ten thousand dollars. When we win, our house will be saved and the town of Hawkins will get all that money!"

Mr. and Mrs. T. shared another long look, and they both nodded as if coming to a decision.

"Okay," they said at the same time.

"Okay!" Cal and Imo shouted back.

Mrs. T. held up a finger. "On one condition," she said. "We have to keep the *fun* in the *fun house* contest. We can't freak out about everything. If it doesn't work, at least we tried. Sound good?"

"Good? That's awesome!" Cal could have jumped up and down, but he just nodded furiously. He didn't want his parents to change their minds.

Imo must have felt the same way. Suddenly she was

all business. "What do we need to do to get started, Cal?" she asked.

"To qualify for this month's contest, we need to complete Stage One in the next two days," Cal explained. "That will be the easy part compared to Stage Two, where we'll have to find a secret treasure hidden in Funland and—"

Waving a hand, Imo said, "Let's take one thing at a time. What's Stage One?"

"We have to get twenty percent of the people in town to sign a sheet saying they 'Like' us," Cal explained. "It's kind of the same as when you click 'Like' online. But here the person just signs our sheet."

"Okay, there are five thousand five people in Hawkins," Mrs. T. said, instantly pulling a fact out of her head. "So twenty percent of that is . . ."

Imo did the math in a flash. "One thousand one. We need to get one thousand one people to give us their Likes in the next two days. That's going to be tough."

"Maybe not," Mrs. T. said. "If the four older Talaskas get two hundred fifty signatures each, Bug can get one. That would be one thousand one right there."

"I'm supposed to play my music tomorrow at the Donegan Diner," Mr. T. said. "I'll see if Ms. Donegan will let me collect Likes while I'm there."

Mrs. T. tapped her chin, thinking. "I'll get mine at the Nate Giacomo *P-A-N-C-A-K-E* Breakfast in the morning."

Nate Giacomo was a famous hockey goalie and one of the athletes Mrs. T. brought to the town to give speeches. The family had to spell *pancake* around Bug. If he heard the word and didn't get one, he might fly into one of his famous tantrums.

"Sounds great," Imo said, tugging her ear again. "I have to figure out where to get my Likes. Cal, how about you?"

But Cal didn't answer. He was already rushing across the patio and reaching for the door to go inside. Cal knew exactly where to go to get his Likes.

And he knew another thing, too, as the handle of the door broke off in his hand.

If the Talaskas wanted to keep their house, they had to win the Funland Fun House Makeover Contest.

The next morning at school, Cal and Imo hurried into homeroom. A couple of years ago, Imo had skipped ahead a grade, so they were in the same fifth-grade class.

They said hi to Ms. Graves, who was at the front of the room erasing yesterday's English lesson off the whiteboard. She was Cal's favorite teacher. She didn't put up with troublemakers, but she let Cal argue about things. Once, Cal convinced Ms. Graves that napping should be an Olympic sport—or at least he *thought* he had, until she started laughing.

Imo headed toward the back of the room with her friend Simone, and Cal took the desk next to his best friend, James, over by the windows. Cal had called James last night to let him know about the contest.

"Morning, Captain!" James shouted, and wiped his nose with the back of his hand. Cal gave him an air fist bump. "You want my Like for the Funland contest now?"

Cal winced and glanced around to see if the other kids or Ms. Graves had overheard James. Luckily, no one was listening. They were too busy unpacking their book bags and getting set for the first bell to ring.

"Easy, my man," Cal said to James. "Whisper. I don't want everyone to know about the contest. The less competition the better."

"Oh right!" James said, still really loudly. "You can have my Like if you want it."

"And I'll give you mine," Cal whispered, hoping James would realize that was how a whisper should sound.

"No thanks," James said. "I'm happy with my house."

James's dad had turned part of their house into a bed-and-breakfast. It was where star athletes stayed when Mrs. T. brought them to town. James said he loved it because it was kind of like living in a hotel.

Cal pulled a clipboard from his bag. The top page was a printout of the Like form he'd found online at the Funland website. The sheet of paper had a bunch of empty blanks for names. "Just sign at the top."

"I'm the first?" James asked.

"That's right." Cal nodded. "After you, I just need to get two hundred forty-nine more to have my share of Likes."

Hawkins was a small town, so all the classes from kindergarten through eighth grade were in the same school. It had the most people of any building in the town—so it was the perfect spot for Cal to get Likes. He planned to spend recess getting all the signatures he needed. There would be plenty of kids left to sign Imo's sheet, too.

As James scribbled his name on the page, the bell

rang. The school day always started with Principal Cahill making announcements over the PA system. But this morning it was the voice of Mrs. Elroy, the school secretary, that came through the speakers.

"Good morning, students!" Mrs. Elroy said. "Principal Cahill would like to make his usual announcements— Oh my!" There was a crash and then the sound of banging. "Unfortunately, Principal Cahill seems to be trapped in the closet in his office."

Ms. Graves sighed from the front of the room. "You're on, Imo," she said.

With a nod, Imo got to her feet. Principal Cahill had the worst sense of direction—and even worse luck. He was always getting locked in rooms, closets, and cabinets all over school. And it was usually Imo who managed to free him. Imo grabbed her tool belt from her desk and headed out of the classroom.

Meanwhile, over the speaker, Mrs. Elroy said, "So I guess I'll do the announcements. . . ." Cal heard the sounds of her frantically shuffling papers. "Let's see, let's see . . . this must be the announcements. . . ." Mrs. Elroy took a breath and started reading. "Messages for Principal Cahill. Mrs. Talaska called this morning to say, 'My son Cal Talaska wants our family to enter the Funland Fun House

Makeover Contest. He and Imo would like to gather Likes from other kids. Is that okay with the school?'"

Everyone looked at Cal. He wanted to shout for Mrs. Elroy to stop, or jump to his feet to do a dance that would distract the whole school.

But he felt frozen in his chair. Mrs. Elroy kept reading the note from his mom. "'If we win as a family, we'll get a makeover for our house on Piedmont Place and the town will get ten thousand dollars. How does that sound? Please tell Cal he has to eat his apple at lunch and that he can't trade it for a candy bar and that his mom loves him!'"

A few of Cal's classmates snickered and made kissing sounds, and Cal turned bright red. Mrs. Elroy continued with the announcements. Actually, she read the school's electric bill, but no one was really listening. Kids were too busy saying stuff like "Don't forget to eat your apple!" and "Don't trade it for candy, Cal!"

"All right, all right," Ms. Graves said. But it wasn't the teasing comments that bugged Cal. He thought they were kind of funny. He was more worried about the serious things he was hearing kids around him say, like "That Funland fun house contest sounds amazing" and "I'm totally going to enter that!"

Cal had been planning to just walk up to people at

recess and ask them to Like him. Now other kids were getting the same idea.

When the bell rang at the end of homeroom, Cal decided he'd better get started right away. On the way out the door, he asked Hank Kirkwood for his Like.

Kendalyn Busque overheard Cal and held up a hand. "Hold on, Hank!" she said. "Don't just give your Like away to Cal!" Kendalyn dug around in her backpack. "Here! I'll give you an orange for it!"

Hank looked confused. "Why can't I just Like both of you?"

"The rules on the Funland site say you can only use your Like once," Cal explained. "And here's why I think you should give it to—"

"Me!" Ayden Parker interrupted. He pushed his way in front of Cal. "Forget the orange, Hank. How about a roast beef sandwich?"

Hank's eyes lit up, and Cal watched him sign over his Like to Ayden. Cal couldn't believe it.

And things just snowballed from there. Now that word had spread about the Funland contest, suddenly everyone in the school wanted to get Likes. A Like was the most valuable thing anyone owned.

During history, a first-grade boy wandered into the

room while Mrs. Fenton was talking about the Great Pyramids of Egypt.

"Hello there, Timmy," Mrs. Fenton said. "Can I help you?"

"Can I have . . ." The little boy swallowed like a nervous baby bird and started again. "Can I have an . . . eraser . . . please?"

Mrs. Fenton looked confused. "An eraser?"

Timmy burst into tears.

Snatching up the eraser from under the whiteboard, Mrs. Fenton thrust it at him. "Here! Here, please take it, it's yours!"

The little guy took the eraser, and as he walked out of the classroom, Cal saw him smile. Cal asked to use the bathroom and rushed out to the hall.

Timmy was just outside the door, sharing a high five with another first grader.

"You were totally faking in there, weren't you?" Cal said to Timmy. "You tricked Mrs. Fenton!"

Timmy shrugged and threw the eraser into a cart. There had to be at least fifty erasers in the cart already.

"What are you going to do with those?" Cal asked.

Timmy grinned wickedly. "Once we have all the

erasers in the school, we'll trade them back . . . for twenty Likes each."

As Cal watched the first graders push the cart toward the next classroom, he had to admit it was a good idea.

An hour later, recess took things to a whole new level of nuttiness. It was a wild Like free-for-all. Kids crisscrossed the playground shouting, singing, and even dancing for Likes.

The kindergartners looked like mini businesspeople marching around with their clipboards. Cal wasn't sure if the younger kids completely understood the contest. They probably just wanted to be part of the excitement.

Even James got wrapped up in it. Cal spotted his friend standing over on the hopscotch grid. He was doing impressions for a Like in front of a tiny audience. James could pretend to be anyone. Right now he was acting like the Head Clown from Funland. No one had

seen the clown in years, but most kids knew him from old Funland commercials on TV.

"We can't wait to make you LIKE us!" James said in the clown's high-pitched voice. The two kids in his little audience clapped.

Cal thought James was smart to use something about Funland to get Likes for the Funland contest. It just made sense. Cal's brain raced through what he knew about the amusement park, looking for his own idea.

Funland was a couple of hours away. That fact didn't help him. Funland had been closed for years. Still no help. Cal knew that when you mixed up the letters in the words *Head Clown,* you got the clown's real name, which was Chad Lowen.

And then Cal knew he had found his idea.

He wrote *I'LL REMIX YOUR NAME FOR LIKES!* on the back of his clipboard and held it up like a sign. At first no one on the playground noticed, but then Cal saw Alison Mangan from his class walking toward him.

"Alison Mangan!" he called to her. *"No slang mania!"*

Confused but smiling, Alison stopped in front of him. "That's true, I guess. I don't have a mania for slang. . . ." She trailed off and waited for him to explain.

Holding out his clipboard for Alison's Like, Cal said,

"I made an anagram for you. I rearranged the letters in your name and turned *Alison Mangan* into *no slang mania*. Get it?"

"That's so cool." She whistled, clearly impressed. "I'd give you my Like, but I'm saving it for someone."

"Who?" Cal asked, disappointed.

"Leslie Wylot," Alison said.

Forget disappointed. Cal was just plain shocked. Leslie was a girl in their class who, like the rest of the Wylots, had been nothing but trouble to Cal, his family . . . and Alison.

Before Cal could say anything else, Alison added, "Actually, Leslie Wylot is a real friend."

"Come on," Cal said.

"No, really," Alison responded. "Now that my dad isn't worried about his promotion at the Wylots' factory, she can't try to control me. She's not so bad."

"Hmm," Cal said. "You're saying she's no longer *sly, low, elite*?"

Alison chuckled at his anagram of *Leslie Wylot*. Cal liked that about Alison. She always laughed at his jokes. "Leslie is missing school because of a dentist appointment today," Alison said, heading over to her friends by the picnic table. "But you'll see tomorrow. I think she's changed."

As Alison walked away, Cal heard shouting coming from the other end of the playground. "Whoa!" Sheila Hanahan was squealing. "Me next! Me next!"

A group of kids gathered around the Rivale triplets, eighth graders who lived next door to the Talaskas. One triplet lay on the ground with his arms extended over his head. He grabbed the ankles of the second triplet. The third did a handstand off the first's shins, and the second grabbed the third's ankles.

It was a complicated setup, but the shape they made was simple:

A wheel.

The Rivales rolled around the playground and offered kids rides for their Likes. As if climbing inside a giant upright tire, kids stepped into the circle of Rivales and stretched out their arms and legs. The Rivales started rolling, and the person inside turned end over end. Even more kids were lining up for a turn.

Seeing the blast the riders were having, Cal realized he needed to step up his game. Anagrams weren't working.

If Cal wanted to win this contest, it was time to unleash the ultimate power of his best talent.

Cal uncapped his pen and crossed out his first sign on the back of his clipboard. Underneath the old message he wrote:

WILL ARGUE FOR LIKES!
You got a problem?
Let me talk you out of it!

Now Cal just had to grab people's attention. He decided to climb to the top of the jungle gym, where everyone would see his sign.

As he hustled over, Emma Wylot stepped in front of him like a ninja appearing out of the mist. Emma held up a hand. Cal automatically ducked, thinking she was going to fire a spitball at him. But she was holding sheets of paper.

"Want a map, Cal?" Emma asked him. Her voice was as smooth as a still ocean. But Cal knew there were always sharks swimming under the surface when she was around. Emma was Leslie's older sister and had gone to scary extremes trying to win the last contest the Talaskas had entered. Cal didn't doubt Emma would do the same today.

The pieces of paper she held had hand-drawn pictures of different parts of the playground.

"Are those maps of the playground?" he asked. "No thanks, I think I know where I'm going."

"But do you?" Emma asked with a wink. "Do you really?" She swept her arm toward the play equipment behind her, and Cal's eyes followed.

Just then two boys playing tag tripped and fell in the sandbox—someone had dug shallow pits in the sand. A seventh grader flew out of a swing—someone had greased the seats of the swings. And a second grader slammed to a halt while going down the slide— someone had put two-sided tape in the middle of it.

Cal was in awe of the chaos Emma had created.

"Booby traps are everywhere," Cal murmured.

"And those are just the ones you can see," Emma said with another wink. "There are lots more. I can give you a map of *all* the booby traps for your Like."

Cal shrugged. "Sorry, I already gave mine away."

Emma stared at him like a spider checking out a fly caught in her web. "Okay, Cal, you can take your chances."

She stepped aside, and Cal walked very carefully toward the jungle gym. He moved an inch at a time and avoided any traps. Imo's best friend, Simone, wasn't so lucky. "Someone" had replaced the rope for the tetherball with bungee cord. The ball spun lightning-fast, and the cord wrapped Simone to the pole like the thread of a cocoon.

Cal glanced at Emma, who was watching him eagerly—as if his next step would trigger his own big surprise. Taking a deep breath, Cal lifted his foot—

"Cal!" a voice shouted. He jumped.

It was Ginny Hollister leaning out of Ms. Graves's classroom window. Ginny was in the fifth grade, too, and she called, "You want a customer, Cal?"

"You bet!" Cal answered. And as he retraced his steps away from the jungle gym, Emma frowned. The fly had broken free of her web.

Cal hustled over to Ginny, who was still poking her

head out Ms. Graves's window. "I'm stuck in here for the whole recess," she said. "If you talk Ms. Graves into letting me out, I'll give you my Like."

Cal looked inside past Ginny to Ms. Graves, who was sitting at her desk. "Is this okay with you, Ms. Graves?" he asked.

Ms. Graves took out her gum and stuck it under her desk. She was always surprising Cal with unteacherly stuff, and that was another reason why she was his favorite teacher.

"All right, Cal, my friend, give it your best shot." Ms. Graves was also the coach of the debate club, so she liked a good argument.

Cal nodded and got down to business. "What's the problem, Ginny?"

"Ms. Graves gave us an assignment to write a paper on a famous American," Ginny explained. "I wrote one about my gerbil. He's famous in my house, and he was born in the United States. I did exactly what Ms. Graves said."

Ms. Graves cleared her throat as if she wanted to jump in, but she kept quiet. "Now," Ginny continued, "I have to spend every recess inside until I redo the paper."

It was a challenge, but if anyone could get the job

done, it was Cal Talaska. "When I get you free," he said, "I get your Like, right?"

Ginny nodded, and Ms. Graves smiled. "Confident," she said. "I appreciate that in an opponent."

Cal got to work. He leaned his head through the window, propping his arms on the sill. He cleared his throat and said, "Tomatoes are a fruit, bananas are a fruit, so is a tomato the same as a banana? When's the last time you put a tomato on your cereal or a banana in spaghetti sauce? When we talk about things, we have to be clear in our definitions. The same is true of the words *American* and *famous*. We have to define what we mean if we expect others to follow our instructions. Otherwise, we'll end up with banana ravioli and chocolate-covered tomatoes!" With that, Cal stepped back from the window dramatically.

"Holy moly," Ms. Graves said, rolling her eyes.

Cal and Ginny waited for her decision. Finally, Ms. Graves burst out laughing. "Fine, fine, go. Anything so I don't have to listen to that line of thinking anymore. Before long, you'll have me believing that famous American gerbils should run for president."

"Thanks, Cal!" Ginny said, and took off toward the classroom door.

"Wait!" Cal called. "I need your Like."

Ginny raced back, leaned through the window, and signed his Like sheet.

"Victory!" Cal crowed, and spun around, holding up his clipboard.

"That's great, Cal," Imo called to him. She was walking out of the school, tucking her screwdriver back into her tool belt. "How many Likes do you have?" she asked, and then she saw his Like sheet. "Oh man, only two?"

"How about you?" Cal asked.

"I've been spending this whole time getting Principal Cahill out of that closet," Imo answered. "He gave me his Like for rescuing him, but that means I only have one. We need to get to work."

Imo was right. Cal was good at arguing, but recess would be over in ten minutes. They needed to get more Likes. And now.

Just then the Rivales rolled by Imo and Cal. Whoops of joy were coming from inside the wheel made by the triplets.

"Is that Mrs. Brenner, the librarian, in there?" Imo asked, stunned.

As an answer they heard a happy shout: "Take me to the library, boys!"

Unfortunately, as the Rivales' wheel was turning toward the school, a fourth-grade boy freed himself from one of Emma Wylot's booby traps. He stumbled out of a sandbox pit into the path of the rolling Rivales.

"Watch out!" Cal shouted.

Too late. The fourth grader looked toward the wheel. He was like a deer in headlights. He froze in place and then—*wham!*

Three Rivales and a librarian mowed over him like a bulldozer over a daisy. The fourth grader was flattened onto the grass.

The Rivales must have felt a bump, because they instantly stopped. But when they did, Mrs. Brenner was upside down. The librarian tumbled onto the grass and got tangled up with the fourth grader.

"Ouch!" they both cried at the same time.

"I'm getting Principal Cahill!" Sheila Hanahan announced, and raced into the school.

Cal helped separate the fourth grader and Mrs. Brenner and got them to their feet.

Everyone was okay, and the Rivales seemed very sorry about the accident. But Principal Cahill was furious. Or at least that was what Mrs. Elroy said over the loudspeakers.

"Attention! Principal Cahill is furious!" Mrs. Elroy cried. Her voice echoed around the playground. "All students, stop what you are doing and listen to this important message from your principal!" There was a *bang!* as if Mrs. Elroy was putting the microphone up against something.

Cal heard the muffled voice of the principal but couldn't make out any words. Everyone on the playground looked at each other, confused. "What is he saying?" Cal asked.

Imo shrugged. "He's probably stuck on the other side of a door or a wall. Again."

Mrs. Elroy came back over the speaker. "Principal Cahill says he wants the town to get the ten-thousand-dollar prize money just as much as anyone. But this Like business is out of control. And he's not going to stand for it!"

Suddenly the muffled talking got very loud. Cal still couldn't understand the words, but it was very clear how angry the principal was.

When Mrs. Elroy spoke again a few seconds later, she sounded a little frightened. "Principal Cahill has an extreme plan to move forward with this contest, and he's warning you . . . you might not *like* it!"

Three hours later, Cal, James, and Imo raced their bikes down Main Street.

They zoomed past Moylan's Gas Station, the grocery store, and the old movie theater. Up ahead, Cal spotted the bright-red hair of Mrs. Swaney, the town clerk.

Outside the library, she had set up a table that was piled high with cupcakes. She was selling them to raise money to fix the town hall's clock tower.

"Sorry, Mrs. Swaney, no time for cupcakes!" James shouted. "We're in a hurry!"

As they zipped by, Cal secretly hoped the clock would never be fixed. He loved Hawkins just the way it was. Even if the Talaskas won the contest and the town got ten thousand dollars, Cal wouldn't want to change a thing.

Except maybe to fix up their house . . . so they could live on Piedmont Place forever, of course.

Imo slowed down on her bike to check out a strange bug on the sidewalk.

"Hurry up, Imo," Cal said. "We don't want to miss Dad's big performance. I'm sure he'll rake in the Likes."

"Um," Imo said doubtfully. "In my opinion . . ." And then she stopped. "Well, anything's better than what you and I got today at school."

Imo sped up, and the three pedaled almost to the end of Main Street.

"Look, Dad's famous!" Cal pointed at the chalkboard in front of the Donegan Diner. Cal recognized their dad's handwriting, and the sign read:

One afternoon only!
Don't miss the musical stylin's and rhymin's of

NELSON TALASKA
The Hawkins Crooner

When Cal lifted his leg to get off his bike, sounds

shot out of the open door of the diner and erupted in the air.

Spart! Sparty! Sparty! Spart! Spart!

Cal blushed, and his friend laughed. "What's that noise?" James asked.

Of course, Cal knew the answer. After all, he was the one who had given the instrument to Mr. T.

"You'll see," he said, and the three of them went into the diner.

The restaurant was packed with customers who were having an early dinner or a late lunch. Cal waved to a few people. Mrs. Moylan, who owned the gas station, sat at the counter, and the veterinarian, Dr. Hanson, was over in the corner booth with his daughter.

But no one was eating. And Cal could see—no, he could *hear*—why.

Wearing his glasses at a slant, Mr. T. was perched on a chair in the center of the restaurant with a table in front of him. On it was the sound effects keyboard Cal had grabbed for him in the Great Grab Contest, and Mr. T.'s clipboard. From where he stood, Cal couldn't see how many Likes his dad had gathered so far.

When Mr. T. spotted Cal, Imo, and James, he grinned and tapped a key on the keyboard.

Ffft! Fffty! Fffty! Ffft! Ffft!

The weird, explosive noises came in a catchy rhythm—but it wasn't the best music to play when people were trying to eat. Diners were glancing down at their food with queasy looks. A few even pushed their plates away.

Then Mr. T. started to sing:

"Like, I'd like your Like if you like,
I'm a Talaska with a big task-a
For a little word I have to ask-a
It starts with L *and ends with* E
All I want is for you to give it to me!
Like, I'd like your Like if you like!"

At home, Mr. T. could really rock his invisible piano on their kitchen table. He said it helped him cope with stress. But when it came to jamming on a real instrument and singing in front of people, it was a different story. Mr. T. could get carried away with the funny sounds, and not everyone was a fan of his off-key voice.

Ms. Donegan was by the cash register, trying to clap along. She was being supportive, but her eyes looked a little panicked.

With a quick goodbye to Cal, James ducked into

the kitchen, where he helped out after school two days a week. His dad was dating Ms. Donegan, and James wanted to be a chef someday.

Flurth! Flurth! Fla! Fla! FLA-FLURTH!!!

Mr. T. had pressed two keys on the keyboard at once. The noises that came out were somewhere between spitting sounds and a really wet sneeze.

Mrs. Moylan gagged a little on her food, and Dr. Hanson asked the waitress, "Can I get this meat loaf to go, please?"

But not all the diners had lost their appetites. In the far corner, Cal spotted a woman he didn't know. She had bobbed brown hair and a plain brown business suit. She stared down at her phone, typing away. Her free hand popped French fries into her mouth while her foot tapped to the music.

"Look, Dad has a fan," Cal said to Imo just as—

HONK! HONK!

The Talaskas' family car pulled up in front of the diner with a squeal of its brakes. What was the Flying Monkey doing here? Cal wondered.

Through the diner's window, Cal saw Mrs. T in the driver's seat. She waved at him and laid on the horn again.

HONK!

"Get in the car, Talaskas!" Mrs. T. shouted. "I'm not sure what the lima is going on, but I just got a call from Sarah the babysitter. We've got a possible BTA on Piedmont Place!"

A few customers gasped. Pretty much everyone in town knew that *BTA* stood for *Bug Tantrum Alert*. Bug was a sweet kid, but he could be extremely stubborn. When Bug didn't get his way, he might turn the kitchen into a mud pit or spin around the grocery store until he threw up. A BTA to the Talaskas was like code red on a submarine. The family leapt into action.

Imo pushed Cal toward the door. "Move, move, move!"

Jumping to his feet, Mr. T. tucked the keyboard and his Like clipboard under one arm.

"Thanks, Janey, hope it wasn't too lame-y," Mr. T. said to Ms. Donegan as he hustled toward the door. For the first time, the diners clapped. Mr. T. didn't notice, so Cal took a little bow for him.

Outside, Mr. T. climbed into the front of the Flying Monkey. "We'll come back for your bikes," he told Cal and Imo. "Here, hold my Likes!"

Cal took his dad's clipboard and squeezed into the back with Imo.

A huge pink plastic cooler took up most of the backseat. "What's in this thing, Mom?" Cal asked as Mrs. T. pulled away from the curb and drove them down Main Street.

Mrs. T. took a deep breath. And then another. "It's been a really bad day," she finally said. "Nate Giacomo didn't show up, and I had to cancel the *P-A-N-C-A-K-E* breakfast."

Giving her arm a squeeze, Mr. T. said, "I'm sorry to hear that, honey."

"Mom, Bug's not in the car," Cal said. "You don't need to spell *pancake*."

"So all the flapjacks from this morning are in here?" Imo knocked on the cooler. "What are you going to do with them?"

Cal had a better question. "Did you get any Likes, Mom?"

"No one came to the breakfast, Cal, so no," his mom said, sounding flustered. "And, Imo, I guess I'll just keep the pancakes in the big freezer in the garage. I'd hate to throw them all away."

"And how about you, Dad?" Cal looked down at his dad's Like clipboard. And answered his own question. The Like page was empty. "Oh no," Cal groaned.

"I played for an hour, not a lot," Mr. T. said. "I think I was just about to get hot."

"Um . . . ," Imo and Cal said at the same time. But they both stopped before saying more.

When the Flying Monkey pulled into the driveway, Bug and Butler were on the front porch, staring up at the babysitter. Once Sarah spotted the car, she waved and tucked her cell phone into her pocket. Everything looked fine.

Then Cal noticed something strange. Sarah was tilted as if she were standing sideways on a hill. Her crazy long hair dangled closer to the floor on one side.

"Sarah, are you okay?" Mrs. T. called as the family hurried out of the car and up the front walk. She was out of breath from rushing around. "Why are you standing like that?"

The answer was obvious as they got closer. Sarah's left leg disappeared into the porch almost up to her knee.

"Totally good?" As always, Sarah said everything like a question when she spoke. "I was just taking Bug and Butler down to the sidewalk when my foot went through the porch?"

Sarah explained that Bug and Butler wanted to set up the card table on the sidewalk in front of the house. They had planned to perform their B&B Spectacular Stunts and get Likes from people walking by.

"I stepped out the front door and my foot just kept going down?" Sarah pulled, but her leg didn't move out of the porch. "Now I'm stuck?"

Crouching next to Sarah's leg, Mrs. T., Imo, and Cal each gave it a tug, with no luck.

"This house has yet another big flaw," Mr. T. said. "Look what it's done to poor Sarah."

Cal felt sorry for the house. "It didn't mean to do it!"

"That's true, Cal," Mrs. T. said. "It's usually a good old place. But right now it's eating the babysitter."

Sarah started laughing. "Oh? Oh? Oh?"

Mrs. T. laughed along with her. "What's so funny?"

Flattening on his belly, Cal peered through the cracks in the floor. Bug and Butler had crawled under the porch and were tickling Sarah's foot—Bug with his hand, and Butler with his tongue. Outside of the family, Sarah was the pair's favorite person on the planet. Cal knew they were worried about her and trying to make her feel better.

"Okay, tickle patrol, that's enough," Mrs. T. said.

With one last tickle, Bug and Butler crawled out onto the front lawn. After a little more chatting about what the Talaskas should do to free Sarah, it came down to a really simple solution. Mr. T. just stood over Sarah, grabbed her under her arms, and pulled her straight up. Her leg slid out smoothly, and Mr. T. put her down gently on the porch. Sarah did a little spin to show she wasn't hurt.

"Are you sure you're okay?" Mrs. T. asked.

Sarah nodded and started down the porch steps, walking very carefully, as if they might collapse.

"Hey, Sarah . . ." Cal hesitated. "Uh, before you go . . . can we get your Like?"

"Cal!" Mrs. T. said. "I think we've put Sarah through enough for the day."

Sarah just laughed. "Bug already has mine? See you next time?"

They waved to Sarah as she walked down the sidewalk toward her house. Imo went to get her tool belt and wood from the garage to fix the hole in the porch. While she was gone, Mr. T. listened to a message on his phone.

A frown touched his face as he took the phone away from his ear. "That was Principal Cahill."

"With everything going on, I forgot," Mrs. T. said. "He called me earlier, too. At least I think it was him. He sounded like he was inside a tin can."

"Probably the supply closet," Imo guessed. She had returned with a board to patch the porch.

Turning to Cal, Mrs. T. put her hands on her hips. "Principal Cahill described what happened today at recess. The librarian ran over a fourth grader?"

"I thought I heard that, too," Mr. T. said. "That can't be true, right?"

Cal looked down at his feet. "Have you ever thought about why you can't tickle yourself?"

"Don't try changing the subject, Cal," Mrs. T. warned. "You were supposed to keep this contest fun and light. Now your whole school is on the brink of disaster!" Her face was getting red. "This is just Stage One, and it's supposed to be easy. What will we do if we get to Stage Two?"

With a big smile, Cal replied, "We're the Prizewinners of Piedmont Place! We'll find the hidden treasure in Funland in Stage Two with no problem!"

Imo tapped a nail to hold the new board in place, then looked up at him. "Thirty-six families have completed Stage One. But no one has ever been able to find the secret hidden treasure."

"That's not super helpful right now, Imo," Cal said. Imo shrugged and went back to hammering nails.

"I'm worried about how tough this contest is." Mrs. T. wandered a few steps away down the porch. "And I don't want you kids getting too upset if we lose."

Cal knew this kind of thinking wasn't like his mom. Mrs. T. used to be an athlete who thrived on the thrills and challenges of the game.

"Mom, I love a little stress," he said. "We all do."

Walking over to her, Mr. T. gave her arm another

squeeze. "Must be in the family genes," he said. "Because you know what he means."

This seemed to bring Mrs. T. back to herself. She patted Mr. T.'s hand. "It's true, we are tough, aren't we?" Her face didn't look as red anymore. She walked back and stood close to Cal. "Okay, let's keep going. So how many Likes did you get today?"

"Two," Cal answered.

"Two hundred?" Mr. T. asked.

Cal shook his head. "No, just two. And Imo got two."

"And Bug got one from Sarah," Imo said, pointing to Bug, who was rolling around in the grass with Butler.

"Your dad and I didn't get a single one," Mrs. T. said. "We have a total of five Likes. We need to get nine hundred ninety-six more in the next day and a half!"

Bug said, "Hgu."

Worried that his mom and the rest of the family would give up, Cal decided it was time to be the quarterback. "We can do it!" he cheered. "Principal Cahill told us about his plan for tomorrow. He says we should be worried . . . but I think it's just what we need to win this contest!"

Principal Cahill had decided that all the Likes given away that day didn't count. Everyone would start tomorrow from scratch. During recess the whole school would go to a Like-Off in the gym. Because spring break started Monday, the principal thought this would be a great way to wrap up the school week.

Tomorrow morning six kids from each grade would form teams. Whichever team got the most Likes during the assembly would get all the Likes in the school to divide up among themselves. Because there were about twelve hundred students, teachers, and staff at the school, each kid on the winning team would get two hundred Likes.

"They're putting out the sign-up sheets at seven-thirty AM in front of school," Cal said. "Imo and I will get on the team for the fifth graders. We'll win and we'll get four hundred Likes, just like *that*!" Cal tried to snap his fingers, but they just made a little squeak.

"Tomorrow's going to be busy enough," Mrs. T. said. "Your grandma Gigi is coming for dinner . . ." She held up a hand before Cal could protest. "But I can probably pick up some Likes at the soccer players' lunch I'm hosting."

"I'll try singing again at the diner," Mr. T. said. "I'll write new songs tonight that the audience will love, and they'll be throwing their Likes at me."

Butler barked, "Rabbo!" and Bug chirped something back.

Imo was tugging her ear—a sure sign her brain was buzzing with new ideas. "I just came up with a genius plan!" she said.

"Don't worry about it, Imo," Cal said. "I've got the idea to end all ideas."

"What is it?" Imo asked.

"Don't worry, you'll see tomorrow," Cal said. "Just one thing. Can I borrow your lawn luge?"

In the morning, Cal waited up in his bedroom for Imo to leave for school first. Wanting his Like-Off plan to be a surprise, he had told Imo that they should each walk to school on their own.

He looked out his window and watched her heading down Piedmont Place. A row of hedges blocked Imo's legs, but she kept glancing down and talking as she went out of view.

Who is she talking to? An imaginary friend? Cal thought. He tried to picture what kind of friend Imo would make up. Maybe a robot spaceship that talked like Jabba the Hutt?

Enough daydreaming, Cal! he told himself. It was 7:00 AM. He needed to get moving to sign up for the fifth-grade Like-Off team. He hustled downstairs to the kitchen and gobbled up a piece of toast with his parents.

Still chewing, he said goodbye and trotted to the backyard and to Imo's workshop. Outside the door, she had parked one of her inventions—a lawn luge. It was a simple wooden board that was longer than Cal was tall. The six wheels underneath made it look like a giant skateboard.

Pulling the rope at the front of the luge, Cal wheeled it across the patio to the garage. He picked up what he needed, put it on the luge, and then headed down the driveway. In front of the house, Bug and Butler were practicing one of their stunts. Luckily, they were too busy running in circles to notice as Cal headed off down the street. Otherwise, Bug would have wanted what Cal was taking to school.

The heavy load on the luge made it slow going at first. But when Cal turned onto Main Street, the road was a little smoother, so it was easier to pull. In fact, Cal moved so fast he almost crashed into one of the town's three parking meters.

He had just reached the school parking lot when the bell in the town hall's clock tower rang. *Dong! Dong! Dong!*

Uh-oh. The clock tower said it was 3:00 AM. It was exactly four and a half hours slow. That meant . . .

It was already 7:30 AM.

Cal had wanted to get to the sign-up sheets at the front of the school much earlier. He left the lawn luge at the side of the building next to the bike rack.

He jogged around the corner, past the KEEP OFF THE GRASS SIGN, and onto the school's front lawn. *BLAM!* A wave of sound as loud as a jet engine slammed into him. Mr. Kelp, the maintenance man, thundered over the grass, seated on his riding mower like a king on his throne.

Uh-oh, Cal thought. He'd have to be fast. Mr. Kelp was very proud of the school's lush green lawn, and he hated when kids trampled it. Luckily, Mr. Kelp was riding away from Cal, so he hadn't spotted him yet.

A couple of hundred yards away, the nine Like-Off sign-up sheets were taped to the wall next to the entrance. James, Alison, Imo, and Imo's best friend, Simone, were already there . . . plus a boy Cal didn't recognize.

In a frightening flash, Cal did the math. There were six slots on each grade's team for the Like-Off, and there were five kids standing in front of his grade's sign-up sheet.

That left one slot for the fifth grade.

He picked up his pace just as a long black limousine pulled up in front of the school. First Emma Wylot and then her sister, Leslie, jumped out of the back and started up the long walkway to the school steps. Leslie's braids whipped behind her like angry tails. She was walking with a kind of determination that told Cal she was here to sign up for the fifth-grade Like-Off team.

All she had to do was beat Cal to the sheet and write her name, and Cal would be out of the contest.

He had to stop Leslie! Before he could think of anything better to say, he shouted, "Wait!"

Somehow Leslie heard him over the blaring sound of the lawn mower. She turned to him and then looked toward the school entrance. Her eyes zeroed in on the five kids standing next to the sign-up sheet.

He knew she was doing the same math he had just done: one slot left.

Leslie waved to Mr. Kelp on his lawn mower to get his attention. She pointed over his shoulder at Cal. Mr. Kelp turned off the machine and shouted, "Get off the grass, Cal!"

"I just—"

"No justs!" Mr. Kelp shook his head furiously. "Last time I *just* listened to you and one of your great ideas,

I took my wife to a drive-in movie on this lawn mower. She wouldn't talk to me for a week after that. I repeat, off the grass, Cal Talaska!"

Mr. Kelp waited for Cal to backtrack to the side of the school and jump off the grass, and then he turned the deafening machine on again.

For Cal to reach the front of the school without walking on the grass, he would have to stick to the sidewalk that wrapped around the lawn. His trip had just been tripled in length.

I've got no choice, Cal thought. He took off sprinting.

Leslie, on the other hand, had all the time in the world. She even stopped and crouched as if smelling a flower next to the sidewalk. He knew she was toying with him. Alison had said Leslie had changed, but Cal didn't think so. Leslie stood and gazed up at the sky as if watching the clouds roll by.

Then she kept walking.

All the while, Cal gained speed. It wasn't enough, though. He was still a hundred yards away.

Leslie stepped in front of the sheet, pulled out her pen, and put it to the paper. But before she signed her name, she stopped and looked at the pen crossly.

It must be out of ink! Cal still had time!

As he turned off the sidewalk and onto the walk up to the front of the school, Leslie reached slowly into her bag and brought out a pencil.

"Wait!" Cal shouted again.

Taking her time, Leslie gave Cal one last wave. Then . . .

She wrote her name on the sign-up sheet.

"No!" Cal raced the final few steps. Imo, Simone, and James spun toward him.

Imo's eyes went wide. "What's wrong with you, Cal? In my opinion, you're acting nutty."

Cal was too out of breath and could only stammer, "I—I—I—"

I am too late, he was trying to say. *I blew the contest.*

Simone must have felt sorry for him, because she gave him a smile. "Hey, Cal," she said. "You know my little brother, Reggie, right?" She pointed at the kid Cal didn't recognize.

"I'm not that little," Reggie said.

"Uh, okay, whatever." Simone laughed and did a little tap dance. She could never keep her feet still. "I guess I should say my *younger* brother."

Cal's brain was catching up to his body. "Wait," he said. "Reggie's not in the fifth grade."

"No, I'm in fourth," Reggie said. "Why does everyone keep reminding me I'm not as old as them?"

"That means . . ." Cal's eyes went to the sign-up sheet for the fifth grade. There was still one slot left. "Quick! Give me a pen!"

"Here you go, Cal," Leslie said sweetly, and handed over her pencil. "Why are you so out of breath?" she asked as he scribbled his name. She must have realized what was going on the whole time.

Now that it was official, Cal could relax a little. "Leslie . . . ," he said, and then couldn't really think of what to say to his archnemesis. "You're here."

"Good deduction, Sherlock," Leslie said with a smile.

"But . . . why?" Cal asked.

"That's a fair question," said Leslie. "It's not like my family needs the money to redo our mansion."

Alison nudged Leslie.

"What?" Leslie said. "It's not bragging if you can Google it." Then she sighed and dropped some of her I'm-the-queen attitude. "Alison said this Like-Off thing is important to her. So . . . that's why I'm here. Because Alison is here. I'm actually the best friend anyone has ever had."

What? Talk about nutty! Cal wanted to shout, and looked at Alison to back him up.

But Alison just smiled. "What? It's not bragging if you can Google it," she said with a laugh, and gave Leslie a high five.

"Okay . . . ," Cal said, feeling like the earth had just shifted under his feet. "There are six of us."

"Thanks again, Sherlock," Leslie said, and stepped forward. "My sister, Emma, and the Rivale triplets just signed up for the eighth-grade team. They're the ones who will give us a run for the money. They've already got a name for themselves: the Like It or Nots."

Cal couldn't stand that bossy Leslie was taking over the group already. Now was his chance to show that he was a great leader. "Oh, that name's nothing compared to the one I just came up with," he said. "We're the Wet Animal Toys!"

Cal was happy for the sound of the lawn mower; otherwise, he probably would have heard crickets.

For once, Simone stopped dancing. "What the heck is a Wet Animal Toy?"

Answering proudly, Cal said, "It's a mix-up of the first two letters of all of our last names. It's perfect because the Head Clown at Funland loves anagrams!"

"Ugh," Leslie said. She looked like she was already sorry about signing up.

"Sounds genius to me," James said, giving Cal an air fist bump. "So, Captain, what's our plan for the big Like-Off today?"

"Yeah, Cal," Imo said, leaning in. "You've had a secret plan since yesterday to win us all the Likes. What is it?"

Even Leslie couldn't help but seem curious. She stopped stroking her braids and peered at Cal.

Locking eyes with each member of the Wet Animal

Toys one after another, Cal let them wait for a couple more seconds.

Then, when he knew they couldn't stand the suspense any longer, he said, "Hold on to your socks."

"Uh, why?" Leslie asked.

"Because if you don't, my plan will knock them right off."

Four hours later, it was almost time for the Like-Off to start.

Cal had been involved in high-stakes contests before. But this was the highest by far. If the Wet Animal Toys didn't win today, Cal and Imo wouldn't get the four hundred Likes. The Talaskas would lose Stage One of the Funland Fun House Makeover Contest—and their house.

Pulling the lawn luge behind him, Cal pushed through the gym's double doors. He felt like he had walked into a carnival. Except the smell of excitement here was mixed with the stench of sweaty socks and forgotten hot dogs in the bleachers.

So far just a few teachers and the fifty or so students

on the Like-Off teams were in the gym. Kids were horsing around or huddled in bunches, plotting how they would nab the most Likes.

Cal looked for the fifth-grade area and dragged the luge past the stage and toward the back wall, where Alison, Leslie, and James waited nervously for him. There was no sign of Imo and Simone.

The rest of the Wet Animal Toys gathered around the luge and the box it was carrying. "Okay, Cal, enough of the mystery, please," Alison said. "What's in the box?"

"My family's secret weapon," Cal said proudly.

Leslie rolled her eyes. "Please don't tell me it's an anagram machine."

Shaking his head, Cal said, "It's something we make better than anyone else."

Leslie seemed ready to say something nasty but glanced at Alison and kept her mouth shut. James opened the lid of the box and peered inside. Then he jumped back and stared at Cal. His eyes were wide with panic.

"Why don't we all do impressions?" James said quickly. He launched into an imitation of the president. "My fellow citizens, your country wants you to give your Like to the Wet Animal Toys!"

"Why are you freaking out, James?" Alison asked.

"What's in there?" She reached into the box and pulled out a frozen disc about the size of a small cake plate. "What are these? Rocks? Bathroom tiles?"

"No," Cal said. "They're pancakes!"

"I knew you could never *take* a joke, Cal Talaska," Leslie scoffed. "But are you *making* one?"

"Come on! Who doesn't love pancakes?" Cal said. "I'll tell you the answer. No one. No one doesn't love pancakes."

"True, but not pancake *Popsicles*." Leslie banged one against the wall. It almost chipped the concrete. "Why are these frozen?"

"The pancakes were left over from my mom's last event," Cal explained. "There are two hundred fifty of them in that cooler. If we get Likes for all them, we're sure to win!"

Why aren't they as excited as I am? Cal wondered.

"Where's Imo?" Alison asked. "She'll know what to do."

Before anyone could answer, the gym quieted down. Kids turned their heads to watch the school secretary, Mrs. Elroy, walk out on the stage. Another woman was right on her heels. Surprised, Cal saw it was the brown-haired woman with the brown suit from the Donegan

Diner. Her head was down, and she typed on her phone with thumbs like woodpeckers as she moved to stand behind Mrs. Elroy.

"Good afternoon, Like-Off teams!" Mrs. Elroy said into a microphone. "Before we begin, if anyone hears Principal Cahill knocking from behind a wall or under a floor, please let us know. Otherwise, let's . . . get . . . this party started!"

Most of the kids clapped and cheered. But not Cal. Where was Imo? She was going to miss the beginning!

Mrs. Elroy tapped the mike to get everyone's attention. "The rest of the school is waiting to come into the gym. Everyone has been given a Like ticket—including you. You can only use your Like ticket once, and you cannot use it for your own grade. The Like-Off will last twenty minutes. Are we ready?"

Mrs. Elroy glanced back at the brown-haired woman, who nodded without looking up from her phone. "Okay, then," Mrs. Elroy said. "On your marks, get set, start Liking!"

The doors were thrown open, and the waiting students and teachers stampeded into the gym. All had red Like tickets in their hands and were looking around as if trying to decide who deserved them.

As kids streamed past the Wet Animal Toys, James tried handing out the pancakes. People either ignored him or jerked away from the frozen pancakes in disgust. "Gross!" one girl said, and another added, "There's not even syrup!"

Desperate, Leslie and Alison started tossing the pancakes back and forth like flying Frisbees. Cal admired their thinking. But no one wanted to even play with this food.

Meanwhile, the other teams were already raking in the Likes.

The sixth graders had created a Smellorama. For a Like, kids could stick their noses into shoe boxes and see what the inside of different students' or teachers' lockers smelled like. The school's best athlete had a locker that smelled like potato chips, and Principal Cahill's had the odor of saltines and sardines.

Cal was relieved to see that the fourth graders were struggling almost as much as the Wet Animal Toys. Their Total Dance Experience promised to create a one-of-a-kind dance move for whoever gave them a Like. Turned out, though, they were pretty bad dancers, and all their moves were exactly the same: It looked like someone standing on one leg and waving goodbye.

Little Timmy and his team of first graders, or Cuties,

as they called themselves, were one of the teams to watch out for. They were Like-grabbing dynamos. The Cuties stood together and made their eyes as big as baby seals'. Then they quivered their lower lips and started to fake-cry.

Anyone who looked their way just handed over a Like ticket, no questions asked. In horror, Cal saw that Ms. Graves was about to walk by the Cuties. He was planning on getting her Like.

"Don't look at their eyes, Ms. Graves!" he shouted.

Too late. Ms. Graves turned and spotted the Cuties.

Their baby-seal eyes were too much for her. "Ohhhhh!" Ms. Graves cooed, and without hesitating handed them her Like ticket.

But the biggest threat by far was the Like It or Nots. There were just four kids on the eighth-grade team—Emma Wylot and the Rivale triplets. Cal figured others in their grade must have been too intimidated to join them, and with good reason. The Like It or Nots moved perfectly together. For a Like, they would transform into any animal, machine, or building kids asked for.

Students shouted "Do a panda bear!" and "Make Bigfoot!" and "Now the Eiffel Tower!"

The Rivales spun through the air like acrobats, and Emma leapt and rolled like a ninja. Cal stared open-mouthed as they made a very accurate version of a beating human heart. Everything they did was in perfect explosions of harmony.

In fact, they performed an actual firework. The Rivale triplets stood on each other's shoulders in a long, tall line reaching up halfway to the ceiling. And then Emma Wylot climbed up their bodies quickly. When she reached the top Rivale, she shot up like a rocket. She did a flip in the air and spread out her arms and legs, making them quiver as if they were the shimmering lights of a firework.

Kids oohed and aahed as Emma seemed to drift back to the ground, where she landed on her feet.

A hand flew into Cal's vision, snapping him out of his daze. It was his classmate Kendalyn Busque. "What are you doing, Cal?" she demanded with her hands on her hips. "You wanted to represent our grade, but you're blowing it!"

"Go, Wet Animal Toys!" Sheila Hanahan squeaked from behind Kendalyn. Cal appreciated her cheer, but Kendalyn was right.

Cal *was* blowing it, and the Like-Off was nearly half over. "The Wet Animal Toys don't have a single Like yet," he mumbled.

"Well, that's about to change!" Imo said. She was striding over to the Wet Animal Toys from the main doors, carrying a large box.

"Where have you been?" Cal demanded. "And where's Simone?"

"Right here, Cal!" Simone called from twenty feet away, and did a little spin.

Imo put the heavy box on the floor at Cal's feet and lifted the front flap. "We've been in the school garage, putting the finishing touches on something."

Crouching next to the opening, Imo said, "Forward."

"What?" Cal asked.

But Imo wasn't talking to him. A remote-control car rolled out of the box. It was the one she had used to dry their clothes after Orca exploded.

Imo had made tons of improvements. She'd painted the car the same purple as the Talaskas' contest T-shirts. On the back, she'd added a plastic box with a slot and a sign that read PLEASE PUT YOUR LIKES HERE! And she'd glued two soft brown eyes and eyebrows to the front of the car, where they bobbed adorably on springs.

"Meet Moose," Imo said proudly. "He's my finest invention ever."

This must be what Cal had seen Imo talking to that morning.

"Why's he called Moose?" James asked.

"Oh!" Imo slapped her forehead as if she'd forgotten something. "The antlers!" She reached for what looked like two long metal branches attached to either side of the car. She swung them up and locked them in place. The metal horns were four feet high.

"Cool!" Alison said. "It does look like a moose! What does it do?"

"It's great at drying wet clothes," Cal said miserably. Things were just getting worse.

"Moose can do something even better," Imo said. "He can save the day. Watch this."

Imo signaled to Simone, who got so excited she did a little jig.

"Hey, Wet Animal Toys!" Simone yelled as if she were reading a line from a play. "Can I get one of those delicious pancakes, please?"

After grabbing one of the pancakes out of the cooler, Imo balanced it on Moose's antlers. Then she leaned over and whispered to the robot, "Forward twenty feet and then come back." Moose jerked ahead and trundled toward Simone. The pancake jiggled, but the horns held it in place.

Cal had to admit that Moose was amazing. "How did you guess my pancake plan and that we'd need a flapjack delivery system?"

Chuckling, Imo said, "You're as hard to figure out as telling the difference between a Wookiee and an Ewok. I knew exactly what your secret plan was the second you asked to use my lawn luge."

"Where's the remote control?" Cal asked. "How are you controlling it?"

Imo pointed at her throat. "Moose listens to voice commands."

All around the gym, kids were stopping to watch as Moose reached Simone. She took the frozen pancake off the antlers. Moose's eyes went cross-eyed and bounced up and down.

Simone held up the pancake and grinned. "Wow, thanks, Wet Animal Toys!"

Imo made a circle with her finger to indicate that Simone should keep going with the playacting. At first

Simone shook her head, but she finally gave in. She bit into the pancake, her tooth clinking off the hard surface.

"Ow!" Simone's hand flew to her mouth; then she caught herself as if realizing all eyes were still on her. "I mean . . . Yum! That's the tastiest pancake ever!"

It didn't matter if her acting wasn't the best. Suddenly everyone wanted Moose to bring them a pancake.

"I'll take one!" Marc Tuminelli shouted, waving his Like ticket, and Carly Lopez called out, "Me too!"

Imo sent Moose out again and again. She would balance a pancake on his antlers and launch him with directions, forward, left, right, and back. After Moose dropped off the pancakes, kids slipped their Like tickets into his glass box.

"He is absolutely incredible!" a seventh grader said to his friend. "Dude, you have to use your Like on this."

As Moose rolled across the floor, his eyes went wider and were even cuter than those of the Cuties. In fact, the first graders' big seal eyes were now slits as they glared at Moose.

Yes, Moose was cute, Cal thought, but he still believed that the pancakes were the true reason for their success. To prove it, Cal bit into one and was instantly sorry. It was like chewing on icy chunks of frozen sawdust.

They were horrible pancakes, but everyone wanted Moose to serve them one.

"Never underestimate the power of an awesome robot, Cal," Imo said as Moose rolled back toward the Wet Animal Toys to pick up more pancakes.

While Imo turned to grab another frozen disc, Leslie leaned down with a wicked smile and whispered to Moose. "Left, left, left, left," she said. Moose didn't move. Leslie tried again. "Right, right, right, right." Still Moose didn't move.

"Sorry, Leslie, you can't make him go in circles," Imo said. "Moose will only listen to me . . . and one other person. I programmed him that way."

"Well, at least someone listens to—" Leslie started to say, but Alison nudged her, and she finished with, "That's neat. You did a good job, Jessie. I mean, Imo."

Wonders never cease, Cal thought.

"One minute left!" Mrs. Elroy shouted from the stage. "If you haven't used your Like, do it now!"

Cal wasn't sure how many Like tickets Moose had picked up. The Wet Animal Toys were flying, but they had gotten off to a slow start. Other teams had been gathering tickets almost twice as long.

"Time is up!" Mrs. Elroy called just as the Like It or Nots created a fully functioning toaster.

Everyone stopped what they were doing. Imo emptied Moose's Like box, and each team sent a representative to the stage with its pile of Like tickets.

Mrs. Elroy and the brown-haired woman sat at a table and tallied the results. Actually, the brown-haired woman never lifted her eyes from her phone, so Cal wasn't sure how she was counting.

As the students waited for the results, the gym went completely silent. The only sounds were from Sheila Hanahan, who couldn't help letting out a squeal of impatience every ten seconds or so. Cal didn't blame her. The suspense was almost too much for him to handle.

Finally, Mrs. Elroy stood up from the table. She walked back to the center of the stage. "We have a winner of the first, and hopefully last, Hawkins School Like-Off!"

This is it, Cal thought. *This is the moment of truth.*

Mrs. Elroy stood up straighter, took a deep breath, and named the winning team.

After the big Like-Off, Cal and Imo took their time walking home from school. The lawn luge was much easier to pull now that it wasn't carrying fifty pounds of pancakes. Moose was riding on the luge next to the empty cooler, his googly eyes wobbling as they rode over cracks in the sidewalk.

"What do you think Mom and Dad will say about today's winning team?" Imo asked, keeping her eyes down.

Cal kicked a rock, sending it bouncing off the curb. "I don't know."

Dragging the luge around the corner, Cal and Imo started down Piedmont Place as three school buses chugged by them.

Up ahead, past the Salmona and the MacGuire

houses, Cal could see their place. The low late-afternoon sun shone off it, making it glow a warm orange. To Cal, this would always be the color of home. He tried to imagine walking down the sidewalk to any other house after school, but he couldn't even let his brain go there. It would be way too sad.

On the sidewalk right in front of the Talaskas', Bug and Butler were performing one of their B&B Spectacular Stunts . . . for no one. From what Cal could see, this was how it went:

Butler ran in circles around Bug while Bug pointed his arms straight up as if he were shooting into the sky. Then Butler would spin away and Bug would pull a pretend cord. He'd jerk his body up and then act as if he were drifting on an invisible parachute.

That was it.

Weird, Cal thought, *even by Bug's standards.*

"Rabbo!" Butler barked when he heard the rattle of the luge's wheels. Tail twirling, he trotted over with Bug. Cal scratched them both behind the ears, and Imo gave Bug a high five.

Picking up on Imo and Cal's mood, Bug stayed quiet as the four headed up the front walk together.

"Let me take care of telling Mom and Dad," Cal

said to Imo as they all went into the kitchen. Their parents were there, doing what they did when they were stressed out. Mr. T. was playing his invisible keyboard at the kitchen table, and Mrs. T. was organizing drawers. They both froze the instant they saw Cal and Imo.

"Well . . . ?" Mrs. T. asked, shaking a sticky note off one finger. "What the cannellini happened?"

"You mean you haven't heard?" Imo asked.

"No, we've been waiting for you to get home," Mr. T. said. "Come on, throw us a bone!"

"Mom, Dad," Cal said. "We don't know quite how to tell you this. . . . Maybe you should come outside."

Nervously, Mr. and Mrs. T. followed them back outside to the porch.

"Just tell us already!" Mrs. T. said.

"Okay . . . if you're ready for it . . . ," Cal said, and then he gave Imo a signal.

"We won!" they shouted together.

The whole family jumped up and down as happy reactions bounced around the porch. "Yarooh!" "Rabbo!" "Top job!"

"Easy, easy!" Mrs. T. stopped jumping and got everyone else to as well. "We're standing right on the spot where Sarah fell through the porch!"

"Come on down and meet the real hero of the day," Imo said, leading the way to the bottom of the porch steps.

Cal thought she was talking about him for a second, but then she lifted Moose off the lawn luge and put him on the front walk. "Moose and his butler routine did the trick," she said proudly.

"Rabbo!" Butler barked at the sound of his name.

"Sorry," Imo said to him. "This time a different butler did it!"

Butler did not seem to like the sound of that. Cal figured he didn't enjoy having a robot replace him as the punch line of the family joke!

Imo gave Moose directions, and he started rolling toward Butler. There was a face-off.

Butler got down on his front paws with his tail high in the air, blocking Moose's path. He kept backing up nervously and murmuring "Rabbo?" as Moose approached.

Trying to help his stunt partner, Bug spoke in gibberish to Moose. "Pots! Pots!" But the robot didn't change his course.

Imo cocked an eyebrow at Bug. "I've programmed Moose so that he only understands regular English from two people."

Cal couldn't resist. He gave it a shot. "Engage rockets!" he said. But Moose still didn't change course.

Grinning, Imo said, "No, it's not you, Cal."

Mr. T. and then Mrs. T. tried talking to Moose. He ignored them and continued rolling along toward Butler. The dog was now leaping from side to side over the robot, just barely clearing the metal antlers.

"Okay, not a good idea," Mrs. T. said. "Looks like Butler kabobs in the making. Everyone inside, please."

"Don't forget, Grandma Gigi is coming over for dinner," Mr. T. said. "We need to get ready and count our Likes to see if we're winners!"

As Mr. T. whipped up his famous meat loaf, Mrs. T. sat at the kitchen table with everyone's Like sheets. She counted up what the family had collected that day. She was lightning-fast and had the results in seconds.

"Cal and Imo brought in four hundred twenty-two Likes from school," she said, "I got two hundred seventy-four at the lunch today, and at the Donegan Diner your dad got . . ." She paused and then started again. "Between your dad and me, we got two hundred seventy-eight. And Bug and Butler have three hundred one."

"*Bug* got three hundred one?" Cal asked, stunned. "Holy Aristotle! How is that possible?" Cal patted Bug's head proudly.

"Well, Bug got the Likes of all our neighbors when they walked by the stunt, including Mr. and Mrs. Rivale," Mrs. T. said. "And three buses of high school kids going on a field trip took a wrong turn and stopped to ask for directions. They loved Bug and Butler and gave them all their Likes."

"So how many does that give us?" Imo asked, and Cal could see that her fingers were crossed.

"We have one thousand one!" Mrs. T. announced. "That's exactly the number we need to win Stage One of the Funland contest!"

The whole family danced around the kitchen, with Bug and Butler performing a waltz. The loose floorboard under their feet let out that beautiful "Hi! Hi! Hi!" squeak that Cal loved. The little party was interrupted by the loud honking of a car.

Hougah! HOU-gah! Hougah!

Imo froze. "Uh-oh. Is that Grandma Gigi?"

"I hope not!" Mrs. T. looked around in a panic. Even Cal had to admit the kitchen was a mess. Pots and pans and dirty dishes were everywhere. "We're not ready for her!"

Grandma Gigi was amazing. But she liked everything to be perfect when she visited from her condo complex for older people across town. The honking continued, and the Talaskas went out to the porch to welcome Gigi.

The tiniest car Cal had ever seen puttered down Piedmont Place. It made their compact Flying Monkey look like the Wylots' limo. This ultra-mini auto was orange and covered in sparkling polka dots. The car stayed on the right side of the street, but it hopped crazily, like it was a beanbag being shaken in a can.

Watching it weave back and forth reminded Cal of the spare tire that had rolled down Piedmont Place the day of their first big contest. That tire had had a message inside written in purple ink, and it had saved the Talaskas' chances of winning that day. They never discovered who had penned that purple note.

The miniature car jerked to a screeching halt in front of the house. Its tailpipe exploded with a *Shuunnng!* and the engine sputtered off.

For a moment nothing moved. Then the passenger door swung open, and a clown wearing a brightly colored tuxedo got out.

"In my opinion," Imo said, "that's not Grandma Gigi."

Another clown emerged from the car. And another. And another.

"Holy Aristotle!" Cal gasped. "It's the Funland Clown Patrol."

The Clown Patrol had been started by Chad Lowen, the Head Clown at Funland. The patrol had been spotted only a few times in the three years since the park had closed for renovations.

Up on the porch, Butler spun with his tongue flapping and his tail whirling each time a clown popped out of the car. Soon there were twelve of them clustered around the empty car—and Butler was one dizzy dog.

"Wait!" Imo said. "It's not empty!"

The brown-haired woman in the brown business suit squeezed out of the car. She had been squished in the backseat. In plain clothes and with her sour attitude, she was the complete opposite of the clowns. Cal recognized her right away—he'd seen her at the Like-Off and over at the Donegan Diner.

"I know that woman," Mrs. T. said. "She was at Randy Russell's speech about the power of soccer today."

The woman didn't lift her eyes from her phone as she shuffled up the walkway to Mr. and Mrs. T.

". . . Like . . . ," the woman said so softly it was more like breathing.

"I'm sorry?" Mr. T. said. "What?"

". . . congratulations . . ."

The Talaskas leaned in closer. Butler's tongue popped back into his mouth, and he cocked his head to the left.

". . . my name is . . ." The woman's voice went even softer, and Cal thought he heard her say, ". . . Dowen . . ."

Mrs. T. must have heard the same thing, because she shook the woman's hand that wasn't holding the phone. "Ms. Dowen, I like that name," Mrs. T. said. "I work with people all the time who don't enjoy public speaking."

"It's true," Imo said. "She had a pole-vaulter who refused to speak on the radio without his pole. Mom convinced him that a toothpick would be just as good."

Ms. Dowen shook her head. ". . . not shy . . . just don't like getting the clowns riled up . . ."

"Excuse me?" Cal said.

With her eyes down the whole time, Ms. Dowen reached into her jacket pocket and removed a penny. She held it up for the family to see and then dropped it on the ground. It was like ringing the dinner bell for a pack of hungry dogs.

The clowns went into a kind of comic frenzy. A few imitated Ms. Dowen dropping the penny, and some acted like it was an explosion that had knocked them off their feet. Others gathered around and pretended that trying to pick up the penny was like lifting the Empire State Building.

Still not looking up, Ms. Dowen raised an eyebrow at the Talaskas as if to say, *See?* She shrugged. ". . . spend all day with them . . . and let me know how you feel about clowns . . . can we come inside . . . ?"

Mr. and Mrs. T. shared a quick look. "Um, sure."

After they had gone into the house, the clowns pushed past the startled Talaskas and began bouncing off the walls—for real. They ran around the house, up and down the stairs, touching and measuring everything with rulers, from the fake fish hanging over the fireplace to Butler's tail.

Because Ms. Dowen was still staring at her phone, Cal almost missed it when she spoke.

"Excuse me?" Cal said.

". . . you are this month's Funland Fun House Makeover Contest Stage One winners . . ."

It was the moment Cal and his family had been hoping for!

But it was also very odd. The Talaskas didn't dare move to celebrate. They were worried that if they made noise, they might miss anything else Ms. Dowen had to say.

". . . or at least we think you are the winners . . . ," she mumbled. ". . . we've been watching you . . . we just need to verify your Likes . . ."

Mrs. T. grabbed their Like sheets and brought them to the living room. Ms. Dowen snapped her fingers and suddenly the clowns surrounded her. She handed the pages to the clowns and they started flipping through them, honking little horns for each Like they counted.

While the clowns worked, Ms. Dowen asked the Talaskas, ". . . what would you like in your new fun house? . . ."

Cal chimed in right away, "A slide from my bedroom to the basement."

Bug said, "Moor tnuts!" Cal had no idea what that meant. Mr. T. said, "A music room," and Mrs. T. added, "A home gym and floors that don't swallow guests."

Ms. Dowen nodded. ". . . find the treasure hidden in Funland in Stage Two and that's what you'll get . . ."

The clowns threw down their horns, and one burst into tears.

". . . or maybe not . . ."

"What's wrong?" Mrs. T. asked.

Without looking up, Ms. Dowen announced, ". . . you have a thousand Likes . . ."

"You mean a thousand and one, right?" Cal said.

". . . clowns don't lie . . ." Ms. Dowen tapped the top Like page. It was Bug's. In the very first spot was a small smudge. Cal squinted and saw that it was part of a paw print.

"Rabbo!" Butler barked as if recognizing the handwriting.

". . . excellent point . . . ," Ms. Dowen said. ". . . but, sorry, dogs do not count . . . you're missing a Like . . ."

"What does that mean?" Cal asked.

But he knew the answer. The Talaskas had not won Stage One after all.

They were out of the contest. And soon to be out of a house.

Just then the doorbell rang. Grandma Gigi had arrived.

"**Q**uick!" Imo shouted. "Lock the door!"

"You can't lock your grandmother out," Mrs. T. said. And then after a split second added, "But I can!"

Mrs. T. lunged for the door and turned the lock.

"What on earth?" they could hear Gigi mutter, and then she pressed the doorbell again. *Ding-dong! Ding—ZZTT!*

"Ow!" Gigi shouted from outside.

"All of you have to hide, Ms. Dowen," Cal said. "Our grandma doesn't have patience for clowns."

With a nod, Ms. Dowen agreed, ". . . who does? . . ."

"Please, you've got to get them out of sight!" Mrs. T.

whispered urgently. "We have some tough news to tell Gigi about the house, and this will just make it harder!"

Ms. Dowen clapped her hands and the clowns scattered. Actually, they capered, romped, jumped, and skipped to different hiding spots in the hall and nearby rooms. Ms. Dowen shuffled toward the kitchen.

Once the Clown Patrol was out of sight, Cal waited for the family to gather behind him. After a quick nod from his dad, Cal opened the door. As it swung open, there was a crash and then a wacky giggle. One of the clowns had thrown himself behind the coatrack in the front hall and knocked it over.

"Grandma Gigi!" Cal shouted extra loudly to cover up any racket.

"Cal," Grandma Gigi said, her dark-brown eyes flashing. As tall as Mr. T., she was thin and angular, with a purple headband pushing back her black hair. She leaned down to give Cal a kiss on the cheek. When she did, she whispered, "You're my favorite grandpup."

Cal didn't get too excited. He knew that when Gigi went to kiss Imo, Bug, and even Butler, she whispered the same thing to them. She loved all of her "grandpups" exactly the same.

"Hello, son," Grandma Gigi said, giving Mr. T. a peck

on the cheek. "Did you know that your doorbell attacked me with an electrical zap? When are you going to have that and this whole place fixed up?"

"You know you can move back here anytime you'd like, Gigi," Mrs. T. said. "Well, here . . . or wherever we end . . ."

Gigi waited for Mrs. T. to finish. Mrs. T. seemed too flustered to go on, so Gigi said, "Thank you, dear, but you know I love my condo over at the mature folks' home." After hugging Mrs. T., Grandma Gigi opened the closet to hang up her coat.

Uh-oh, Cal thought. He was sure there was a clown hiding in there.

"Let me do that for you," Mrs. T. said.

"I've got it, dear," Gigi insisted. She slipped her coat onto a hanger and thrust it onto the rack in the closet. There was an *umphh* from the clown. Cal cringed, waiting for Gigi to react, but she didn't say a word. Instead, she closed the door and led the way into the living room.

"Seems like you might have changed some things around," Gigi said. Cal knew she wasn't a fan of change.

"Um, not really," Mrs. T. said.

"Oh, I think this couch used to be against the wall,

wasn't it?" Gigi asked. "Like this?" She gave the arm of the couch a shove, pushing it back toward the wall. As the couch slid, another *umphh* from a squished clown filled the room.

Still Grandma Gigi didn't react. She took a seat on the couch and stared at the family as if waiting for something. Finally, she turned her full gaze on Mr. T. "What are you up to, son?"

Mr. T.'s face got red. "What do you mean, Mom?" He pointed at an old picture of him and Mrs. T. on the wall. "Remember when we went to prom?"

But Grandma Gigi wasn't going to be distracted. "If you want to play a game, I can do the same."

She shifted again on the couch, pushing it back a little more with her feet. This time there was a much louder *umphh*.

Gigi cocked an eyebrow at Mr. T., who sat silent. She sighed as if she didn't want the evening to come to this but she had no choice.

"I brought you a present," Gigi said loudly, and held out her hands.

Bug jumped to his feet at the word *present*. But he plopped back down when he saw that Gigi's hands were empty. She was playing a game.

"I brought you a giant boa constrictor," Gigi announced, acting as if her arms were full. "Isn't he a beauty? But I'm worried because he's so hungry and might just eat anything or anyone. Why don't I put him in the closet for now?"

Getting to her feet, Gigi clomped loudly over to the closet door in the front hall. Just as her hand was reaching to turn the knob, three clowns rushed out in a panic.

Gigi still didn't react. She walked back into the living room and pulled the window curtain aside. Four more clowns tumbled to the floor.

Calmly, Gigi took a seat on the couch. "Why is this house stuffed full of clowns?"

"Grandma Gigi," Cal said, "this is the Funland Clown Patrol, and this is Ms. Dowen. . . . Ms. Dowen, you can come out now, please."

Ms. Dowen stepped out of the kitchen. She shook her head and said something that no one could hear.

Cal explained, "Ms. Dowen and the clowns are with the Funland Fun House Makeover Contest."

Mr. T.'s eyes went wide. He was clearly trying to tell Cal not to talk about the contest.

"I've heard about this nonsense," Gigi said.

"Really?" Cal asked.

"My friends have grandchildren who have been asking me for my Like all day," Gigi said. "What does that even mean? *Like?*"

Cal suddenly felt a spark of hope. But he had to play it just right. Gigi didn't enjoy being rushed. "The family that gets a certain number of Likes will get a chance to search for a hidden treasure in Funland. If they find that, they'll have their house fixed up. We're just one Like away from getting our chance!"

Grandma Gigi's eyes flashed. She turned to Mr. T. "This is the way you're going to save the house you grew up in—the house *I* grew up in? With a bunch of clowns? No offense." She said this last part to the clowns, and the nearest one to her honked his horn to let her know there were no hard feelings.

Ms. Dowen headed toward the door. ". . . we were just leaving anyway . . ."

"No, you aren't," Gigi said, and held out a hand to gently stop her. "My dear, I may come across as strong, but no one has ever accused me of being rude. At least not to my face. Please take a seat. That goes for everyone."

In a flurry of movement, the clowns acted as if they were having a seat in invisible chairs. One pretended to be on a ski chairlift and glided around the room.

One acted as if she were on a bouncy ball and careened off the furniture. Six of the clowns turned themselves into a throne and motioned to Miss Dowen that it was for her.

Ms. Dowen just ignored them, but her face looked pained. ". . . they do this . . . all . . . the . . . time . . . ," she said to the Talaskas. ". . . we really have to go . . . have to find a winner of Stage One . . ."

"Wait," Cal said. "Please!"

Mr. and Mrs. T. tried to convince Ms. Dowen to stay, too. But it was no use. She waved goodbye and, with the Clown Patrol right behind her, walked out the front door.

Cal collapsed onto a chair. He didn't know what to do. They had been so close to completing Stage One—just one Like away—and now they had nothing!

The rest of the Talaskas must have felt the same crushing disappointment. They sat in the living room with Gigi, staring at each other as the clock on the coffee table ticked.

On top of everything, Cal felt sure that Gigi was about to explode. She must be furious that they had been wasting time on a contest instead of finding a real solution to save the house.

When Gigi slowly reached for one of the Like papers that a clown had dropped, everyone else jumped a little. But Gigi just calmly flipped over the page and started doodling on it with a pen she took from her purse.

Two minutes passed and still no one spoke. Finally, Grandma Gigi said, "Cal, can I ask you a question, please?"

Uh-oh, Cal thought. But he nodded.

"How long do you think it takes thirteen people to put themselves back into a car the size of a toaster?" Gigi asked.

"I don't know, five minutes?" Cal guessed.

"Hmm," Gigi said. "Sounds about right."

She went back to her doodling. The clock continued to tick.

After another two minutes, Gigi recapped her pen and put it back in her purse. "Well, it's been four minutes and fifty-five seconds since the clowns left the house," she said. "So they should still be out front when you bring them this."

She held out the Like sheet to Cal. Cal looked down at what she had been drawing. The picture showed a bedroom with a merry-go-round in it.

"That's what I'd like to see in my room next time I'm here," Gigi told Cal.

She gestured for him to flip over the page. On the other side, she had signed her own name next to Butler's paw print.

Gigi had given the Talaskas the last Like they needed.

But what shocked Cal the most was that the doodle and her signature had all been made with purple ink. It was the same as the ink used in the message in the spare tire that had saved the day in their first contest.

Gigi saw his eyes widen. She held her finger up to her lips. "That's just between us, grandpup." Then she leaned in and gave him another kiss on the cheek. "Bring me back a souvenir from Funland!"

With whoops of joy from other family members ringing in his ears, Cal raced out the door to stop Ms. Dowen and the Clown Patrol before they left Piedmont Place. If he ran fast enough, he knew he'd catch them.

The next morning, Cal sat straight up in bed before even opening his eyes. It was as if his body was too eager to waste time on lifting his eyelids—and wanted to get moving right away!

Normally at this time of year, Cal would be excited no matter what. After all, it was the first day of spring vacation. Even better, the Talaskas were about to have a vacation that other families could only dream of.

Cal wondered if he should wake up the rest of his family. Last night when he had caught up with the Clown Patrol, Ms. Dowen had made it clear that the Talaskas had to be ready at noon. She had a special surprise for them to kick off Stage Two of the Funland Fun House Makeover Contest.

The family would soon be on their way to saving their house!

But first Cal had to save himself . . . from Butler's breath. Even from across the room where Butler was curled up and snoozing in Bug's bed, the smell was strong enough to peel paint.

Plugging his nose, Cal opened his eyes and found a pile of clothes at the side of his bed that Mr. or Mrs. T. must have left for him while he was sleeping. It was his purple shirt and his purple belt. Everyone in his family had similar clothes—they were the family's costume that had brought them so much luck in their first contest.

Cal slid out of bed and put on a pair of pants, his purple belt, and the purple shirt.

"Let's go, Bug!" Cal told his brother on the way out of the bedroom. "Time to conquer Stage Two!"

He heard Butler give a sleepy "Rabbo" and Bug mumble something like "Ces a ni."

Downstairs, the kitchen was quiet. Cal decided if there was ever a day that needed to be powered by pancakes, it was this one. He was pulling out the ingredients they'd need to get them started as the rest of the Talaskas trickled in.

Everyone had the smooshed bedhead that Grandma

Gigi called "hairdo by pillow." In her purple shirt and orange sweatband, Mrs. T. was rubbing her eyes. She stopped him from taking a jar out of the refrigerator. "Olives, Cal?"

He shrugged. "I was going for something a little different for the pancakes today."

"Thanks, honey. Why don't you just grab the spatula for me?"

Once the Talaskas had gobbled up the regular-flavored pancakes and cleaned the kitchen, they still had three hours to wait until Ms. Dowen arrived to start Stage Two and take them off to Funland. The family sat in the living room to do something that Cal found almost impossible:

Wait.

Mrs. T. was at her desk near the fireplace, clicking away on her keyboard. Every now and then she'd say "Hmm" and "Well!" as she gathered trivia facts about Funland. Mr. T. was playing his invisible keyboard on the coffee table. Imo was out back in her workshop, banging and hammering on a new invention. And Bug and Butler were spinning in circles together on the rug. Butler was moving so fast that his purple collar was a blur.

With every sound he heard, Cal leapt to his feet

and ran to the window to see if Ms. Dowen was early. But the first time, it was Mr. Salmona out clipping the hedges down the street. The next time, it was a squirrel rustling around in a pile of leaves. And the last time he ran to the window, there was nothing.

"Cal!" Mrs. T. finally said, and rubbed her eyes again.

"You need to go out and run around," Mr. T. said. "You're making everyone nervous with all the jumping up and down."

But Cal wanted to save his energy. They were going to need every ounce of it to track the hidden treasure when they got to Funland.

After what seemed like an eternity—

HOU-GAH!

The honking sound at exactly noon was sweet music to Cal's ears. Ms. Dowen and the Clown Patrol were heading down Piedmont Place!

The Talaskas hurried out the front door, carrying their luggage. They didn't know how long it would take them to find the hidden treasure at Funland, so they had packed extra pairs of underwear and their toothbrushes. Imo had even packed Moose back in his box for the trip.

A bus and a tow truck—both bright orange with polka dots—were waiting for them on the street. The bus went on for nearly half the block and had two giant hinges in the middle.

"Those are so the bus can make it around turns," Imo told Cal.

Along the side, a digital sign as long as the Wish Shoppe billboard flashed the message FUNLAND! LIKE US! LIKE US!

The bus door opened and Ms. Dowen stepped out to greet them ". . . ready to go? . . ." she asked.

"Absolutely!" Cal couldn't wait to check out the inside of the bus.

Without looking up, Ms. Dowen held out her phone to stop him. ". . . Like this first, please. . . ."

The Talaskas leaned in to read the small screen. There were pages and pages of contest rules, and Mr. T. had to keep swiping and swiping until they reached a button at the end that said LIKE.

Mr. T.'s finger hovered over the button. He seemed unsure.

"What do the rules say, Dad?" Cal asked. He had stopped reading after the first six swipes.

"Basically, we have to follow the contest rules to the letter," Mr. T. said. "But we can quit anytime if we think that's better."

With a nod from Mrs. T., Mr. T. clicked LIKE.

As if Ms. Dowen were starving and the phone were a sandwich, she snatched it back from Mr. T. ". . . the tow truck will take your car to Funland . . . but we want you to arrive in style . . ."

She stepped aside and motioned to the Talaskas to board the bus. Big overstuffed furniture, a kitchen stocked with snacks, a bathroom with a hot tub, and what looked like a one-lane bowling alley awaited them. They took a seat on a plush couch facing the windows. As the clown bus driver pulled away from the curb, Cal took one last look at their house.

Next time I see you, Cal thought, *we'll have won the contest and you'll be safe.*

Cal's family seemed to be thinking the same thing. They were all looking back at the house.

"Funland, here we come!" Cal said.

". . . with one stop first . . . ," Ms. Dowen said. ". . . I've invited your town to see you off and tell you how they want to spend the ten thousand dollars if you win. . . ."

This was getting better and better. Cal couldn't wait for his friends to see him on this mega-monster of a bus. The bus cruised into town and stopped in front of the town hall.

A banner that read TELL A TALASKA WHAT YOU WANT! hung between two light posts. And everyone in Hawkins was standing on the stone steps leading up to the building.

A few people were holding up signs that read SAVE

THE CLOCK TOWER! and BUILD A NEW DONUT SHOP! and GIVE EVERYONE $2! and GIVE ME ALL THE MONEY!

Not surprising to Cal, that last sign was held by Leslie Wylot.

"Looks like everyone has an idea how the town should spend the ten thousand dollars if we win the contest," Mrs. T. said.

"Imo, there's Simone!" Cal said. But Imo stayed off to the side. She hated anything to do with being in front of a camera or being up onstage.

Alison Mangan waved her own sign, which read GO, WET ANIMAL TOYS, GO! And next to her was James.

"Hey, James!" Cal said, and knocked on the window. But James didn't seem to hear him.

Butler leapt up on his hind legs and pressed his front paws against the glass. "Rabbo!" he barked. No one outside noticed him, either.

"They can't hear us through the glass," Cal said. "Can we get off the bus to say hi?"

Ms. Dowen shook her head. ". . . no time . . . special windows . . . they can't hear you . . . but do you want to hear them? . . ."

Ms. Dowen typed on her phone. In the reflection of

the town hall's windows, Cal saw the message on the side of the bus change.

It now read TELL THE TALASKAS HOW YOU WANT THEM TO SPEND THE $10,000 PRIZE MONEY ON YOUR TOWN!

There was some jostling in the crowd on the steps as Mr. Wylot rudely pushed his way to the front. "I can't always be the one writing checks around here," he grumbled. "I think the money should be used to make a statue of one of the founders of Wylotville—"

"Oh brother," Mr. Mangan said. "We're not changing the name of the town to *Wylot*ville, Mr. Wylot. And your family hasn't been here any longer than anyone else." Cal was impressed with Alison's dad for standing up to Mr. Wylot. Most people just did whatever Mr. Wylot said.

"The clock tower!" Mrs. Swaney squeaked. "Save the clock tower!" But no one was listening.

With her head still down, Ms. Dowen typed on her phone.

"Are you changing the message on the bus again?" Imo asked her. "What are you writing?"

". . . what your family thinks of the town's ideas . . ." Ms. Dowen pressed a button.

"I'd love to go outside and thank everyone—"

Mrs. T. started to say with a smile. But her smile disappeared when she saw the faces of the crowd change. They were reading the new message on the bus, and many gasped in surprise.

"Typical of those Talaskas," Mr. Wylot said, pointing at the side of the bus.

In the town hall's windows, Cal could see the reflection of the flashing message. It was a long one, and it took a second for his brain to take in what he was reading.

WE'LL SPEND THE MONEY HOW WE WANT! KEEP YOUR IDEAS TO YOURSELF!

Oh man! Cal thought. *That's awful!*

"Wait!" Mrs. Talaska cried. But Ms. Dowen clapped her hands once, and the clown driver slammed his oversized shoe on the gas pedal. The bus lurched forward, and the Talaskas were thrown back onto the couch.

Imo turned to Cal. "You wonder why I don't like talking in front of people?" she said. "That's why!"

Mrs. Talaska asked, "Why the fava did you do that, Ms. Dowen?"

". . . people like confidence . . . ," Ms. Dowen said. ". . . research shows people like jokes . . . leave them laughing . . ."

That wasn't a very good joke, Cal thought, *and people definitely weren't laughing.* As the bus barreled down Main Street, Cal could see that many Hawkinsites were still stunned. Others were walking away, shaking their heads. Emma Wylot had shinnied up the light pole to pull down the banner.

This wasn't the way Cal wanted to win. "Those people are our friends!" he said.

". . . they'll *like* you even more when you find the secret treasure and win the contest . . . ," Ms. Dowen said.

Mrs. T. reached for her cell phone. "We'll just call our friends and apologize."

". . . when you get back home in five days . . . ," Ms. Dowen said. She explained that according to the rules, the Talaskas were not allowed to use their cell phones to contact anyone until the contest was over. What they were going see at Funland was top-secret and couldn't be shared with anyone else.

"This is too much," Mr. T. said. "I've never heard of such—"

". . . if you want out of the contest now . . . that's fine . . ."

"No, no," Mr. T. said "It's just so . . ." He trailed off.

Cal knew the family didn't have much of a choice. He just hoped James and everyone else in Hawkins wouldn't be too mad at them when they got back home. It was just one more reason the Talaskas had to win— the ten thousand dollars would make a great apology!

The drive to Funland Amusement Park took just over two hours. On long family trips, Bug would usually demand to stop at every rest stop, even if he didn't have to go to the bathroom. He loved looking at the pictures that showed tourist attractions in the area.

Even with all the gadgets and games on the bus, Mr. T. must have worried that Bug would throw a tantrum if he saw all the rest stops whizzing by. Trying to distract him, Mr. T. put his hands on an invisible keyboard in front of him and wrote a goofy song titled "Funland, You're Better Than a Disco Band!"

Finally, the bus pulled into a parking lot that had to be the size of at least five football fields. But there was only one tiny car parked in it.

Cal was glad to see the Flying Monkey, even if it did look a little lonely.

". . . welcome to Funland . . . good luck . . . ," Ms. Dowen said, and hustled off the bus. Imo grabbed Moose, and the Talaskas quickly followed Ms. Dowen.

But when they stepped outside in the bright afternoon sunshine, it was as if she had vanished. There was no sign of her, only the high walls that ran around Funland.

"Where'd she go so fast?" Imo asked, setting Moose down on the pavement.

The door closed and the bus raced out of the parking lot—with all the Talaskas' luggage.

"What do we do now?" Cal said, and watched his family's eyes turn to the Flying Monkey. He knew they were thinking about getting inside and driving back home. But they wouldn't have a home for long if they didn't stay.

"We have to see this through," Cal said, and he led the way toward the main gates of the park.

As they got closer, the gates opened a crack with a squeaky lurch. The Talaskas had crept forward to peer inside when—

A clown in a tuxedo and a top hat somersaulted out of the narrow opening. He flipped twice in the air and landed directly in front of the Talaskas.

"Why, hello!" the clown bellowed in a deep voice, and held out his hand as if waiting for something. Cal and his family just stared blankly at him and his empty hand.

"Here's a hint," the clown said. He reached out and brushed a feather against Bug's chin. Bug giggled and squirmed. "Tickle tike!" the clown cried.

Mrs. T. moved herself between Bug and the clown. But Bug didn't seem to mind the tickling.

"*Tickle tike* is an anagram, Mom," Cal said. "He means *Like ticket.*"

"Oh! Here you go." Mrs. T. pulled out their Like sheets from her bag.

The clown took them. "Your Likes are your ticket into the park!" he shouted. "Are you ready for the most fun of your lives in Funland?"

With the clown leading the way and Moose rolling next to Imo, the family walked through the gates.

Up ahead, a high platform would normally have given them a view of the entire park. But a giant movie screen blocked their way. The screen flashed, and a face the size of a house popped up. The face was hidden in shadow and spoke in a voice that sounded like a computer. It reminded Cal of one of James's impressions.

"HELLO!" the face said.

The Talaskas jumped at the loud voice, and Bug said, "Olleh!"

"Welcome to Stage Two of the Funland Fun House

Makeover Contest!" the face said. "Your mission is to find the hidden treasure in the Funland Amusement Park in the next five days."

"What is the hidden treasure, anyway?" Imo asked, more to herself than anyone.

But the face seemed to hear her. "What's the hidden treasure, you ask? Is it gold? A new car? Diamonds?"

With each word, Cal got more excited. Then the face said, "No! It's way better than all of that. The hidden treasure is a BLUEPRINT!"

"A blueprint?" Mrs. T. asked.

"No, a BLUEPRINT!" the face cried. "I can tell you're not saying it right. It's in all capital letters. As you know, a BLUEPRINT can be the plan to create new buildings or do a home makeover."

The screen showed what looked like a rolled-up poster. The poster unspooled and lay flat. On it was a drawing of how a house should be built.

"Um . . . ," Cal said. They were looking for a piece of paper? That didn't sound very exciting.

"Don't be disappointed!" the face said. "Our BLUE-PRINT is different. It's a way you can create your fun new future! Find it in the park in the next five days and you will win the contest!"

The screen went dark and sank into the ground. Without it blocking their view, the Talaskas could see almost the entire amusement park.

But what Cal saw actually made him stumble. His stomach sank and his head felt dizzy. He couldn't believe his eyes.

"What the kidney bean?" Mrs. T. exclaimed.

Funland looked like it had been run over by a bulldozer.

No, Cal thought, *make that a thousand bulldozers.*

From where the Talaskas stood, the park spread out below them. What was left of the park, anyway. Rubble and destruction were everywhere.

"As you can see, we're undergoing a very slight makeover," the clown in the top hat said. "Doesn't it look FUN?"

"Uh . . . ," Mrs. T. said, stunned.

So this was the reason the park owner was so secretive, Cal realized. Not because Funland had amazing new rides but because it had barely any at all.

A few were operating. The blimps on high wires that served as transportation still crisscrossed the park. And over in the distance, the world's tallest Ferris wheel continued to spin.

But demolition was just about everywhere else in all five sections of the park. The center of Pharaoh's Kingdom looked as if it had been flattened by a fleet of steamrollers. Over in Haunted Land, construction clowns were tearing apart Ghost Mansion and the Ghastly Ghoul Roller-Coaster Ride with jackhammers and a wrecking ball. In the last three sections—SportsWorld, StarVille, and Runaway Train—clowns were smashing and blowing up a skateboard boat ride, a Martian restaurant, and the Day Before Tomorrow Pavilion.

Above all the destruction and looming on the hill just opposite the park's entrance was Clown Castle, home of Chad Lowen, Head Clown.

"Do you LIKE what you see?" the clown in the top hat asked. He sounded nervous.

"Uh . . . ," Mrs. T. repeated.

Still in shock, Cal turned to the clown. "Are you the Head Clown? Are you Mr. Lowen?"

The clown laughed. "No, I'm Mr. Pottah. I'm your Clown Butler, and I'm not alone!" He clapped his hands, and the Clown Patrol popped out from behind garbage cans, under manhole covers, and inside hollowed-out tree trunks. Dressed in tuxedos, like Mr. Pottah, they danced and jiggled around the Talaskas.

"During your stay here, we'll all be your Clown Butlers!" Mr. Pottah said.

"That's the name of our dog," Imo told him.

Mr. Pottah patted Butler on the head. "Why, hello, Clown Butlers!"

Bug said something, and Imo translated. "No, it's just Butler."

"Aha!" Mr. Pottah said. "That makes you the perfect family for this contest! It's going to be an even bigger shame when you don't win!"

Whoa, Cal thought. "We have to win! If we don't, we'll lose our house."

One of the clowns burst into tears.

"That's the saddest clown I've ever seen," Mrs. T. said.

"It's been tough on us during the years since we closed," Mr. Pottah said. "The thirty-six families before you failed to find the BLUEPRINT in Stage Two. Please, please, will you be the ones to say they did it?"

The family all looked at each other, and to break the tension they all said at the same time, "Did it? The Butler did it!"

Mr. Pottah looked down at his shoes as if he might have stepped in something.

"Um," he said, "let us show you to where you'll be

living for the next five days." He led the way down SuperFun Street, Funland's version of Main Street. The shops and restaurants on both sides were either half-way destroyed or boarded up.

"I guess we won't be getting Grandma Gigi a souvenir after all," Imo said.

Cal shrugged. "As long as we have a house, that's all she'll care about."

"You're allowed to go anywhere in the park!" Mr. Pottah explained. "If you get lost, just look for the Lamppost of Fun and you'll know you're home!"

Up ahead, Cal could see the lamppost. It was shaped like a tall, skinny clown wearing a butler outfit and a top hat. The top hat contained a giant lightbulb, which shone bright even in the day.

The pack of clowns that had been swarming in front of the Talaskas suddenly parted like a curtain, and Mr. Pottah cried, "The famous Funland Fun House!"

"Holy Aristotle," Cal breathed. He couldn't believe he was actually seeing it in person. Still in one piece, the fun house rose four stories and was as long as two basketball courts. The statues of the T. rex and the brontosaurus were battling next to the dinosaur waterfall—just like the clay models Cal had made in his basement.

After dancing over to the feet of the T. rex, Mr. Pot-tah held out a hand and dangled a set of keys.

Cal squinted. "Are those car keys to the Flying Monkey?"

With a nod, Mr. Pottah tossed the keys twenty feet into the air. They jangled as they turned end over end and landed in the T. rex's mouth. The dinosaur's jaws clamped shut with a *whomp!*

"The keys will stay locked inside there until your five days are up," Mr. Pottah said. "If you quit early, we'll take you home on the bus." He waved at someone behind the Talaskas. "Thanks, Declan!"

Cal looked around and spotted a short clown standing behind a control panel. He must have been making the T. rex's mouth move.

"Now I'll take you to your rooms." Mr. Pottah walked up the steps of the fun house.

"Excuse me? Our rooms?" Mrs. T. said. "We can't live in a fun house for five days."

Mr. Pottah seemed surprised. "Why not? We've got extra clothes for you inside, we'll bring around a snack truck for your meals, and there are more restrooms in the park than you could possibly ever use!"

"But this is a ride!" Imo said.

"I might be a clown, but I know what that says," Mr. Pottah said, pointing to the FUN HOUSE sign. "Fun? Yes! House? Yes! And according to their comments online, people like FUN and people like HOUSES! So what's not to like?"

"I . . . ," Cal started, and trailed off. Even he wasn't sure how to argue against such strange logic.

"Plus," Mr. Pottah added, "we tore down the hotel last week because we got a mean comment about it from a six-year-old in Funafuti." He slapped his hands together as if it were a done deal. "There really is no other place for you to stay in Funland. And now for the family photos!"

The butler clowns reached into their baggy pants and pulled out huge cameras. They started snapping pictures of the Talaskas, the camera lights flashing wildly.

"What's this?" Imo asked, terrified.

"If you win, which you probably won't," Mr. Pottah said in a cheery voice, "we'll take pictures of you going into your made-over house. This is just practice. Strike a pose!"

Practice or not, Cal knew this was Imo's nightmare. To get the cameras to point away from her, she spoke to Moose. The robot started spinning, his eyes wobbling and his antlers bouncing up and down.

Her plan worked—the clowns focused on Moose.

The opposite of Imo, Bug wanted all the attention for himself and Butler. To get in on the act, Bug leaned over and whispered something to the dog.

"Rabbo!" Butler barked, and he spun like Moose, turning faster and faster until the dog and the robot crashed into each other. Butler bounced off and knocked into the Lamppost of Fun.

With a *crack!* an object broke off the lamppost. It fell through the air and landed in Moose's Like slot. *Thwick!*

The clowns stopped taking pictures. Cal could see Mr. Pottah turn pale, even through the clown makeup.

"Oh, kids," Mrs. T. said, embarrassed. "Don't tell me you've already broken Funland!"

Imo tried getting the object out of Moose with pliers from her tool belt. "It's jammed in there pretty good," she said. "I'll have to wait until we get home to my workshop to get it out. I don't want to crack the glass case."

"Probably a souvenir that someone forgot about." Cal crouched to get a closer look. "It's a pin shaped like a butler. Can we keep it and give it to our grandma, Mr. Pottah?"

The clown just stared at the pin. As if he knew exactly what it was and it meant something to him. Then he snapped out of it.

"Whatever you want!" Mr. Pottah said. "Just as long as you LIKE us!" Then he clapped his hands again, and the clown paparazzi tucked their cameras away. "Get a good night's rest, Talaskas, because starting tomorrow you have to, um . . ."

When Mr. Pottah trailed off, Cal said, "Find the BLUEPRINT?"

"Yes!" Mr. Pottah nodded frantically. "Because the

rules say, find the BLUEPRINT in five days and you'll win the makeover! Goodbye!"

With that, Mr. Pottah and the pack of clowns hustled down SuperFun Street.

The Talaskas were left alone in front of what would be their home for the next five days.

"**W**ell, let's check it out!" Cal said. He led the way past the dino waterfall and into the fun house. The walls of the first room sparkled and shimmered under bright overhead lights. Sniffing the ground, Butler trotted ahead, and *blam!* He bounced off an invisible force field.

Not a force field, Cal realized, but glass. The family was in a hall of mirrors. It was a maze. The mirrors spun ever so slightly so that the path was constantly changing.

"Everyone stay close," Mrs. T. said.

But the Talaskas got split up anyway as they wove through the mirrors. When Cal finally found his way out of the hall, he was alone in a room the size of his bedroom at home.

"Hello?" Cal called, moving to the center. "Mom? Dad? Im—"

Phlit!

A trapdoor opened under Cal's feet and he shot down a polished wooden slide. After falling two stories, he plunged into what he guessed must be the deepest, softest ball pit on the planet.

With a *whoop!* he popped to the surface. "You've got to try this!" he shouted to his family—wherever they were.

"Do you like it, Cal?" Mr. Pottah's voice came from a nearby speaker.

"I love it!" Cal responded.

"But do you LIKE it?" Mr. Pottah asked again.

Cal wasn't sure exactly what the clown was getting at. "Um, I guess . . ."

"That's all we need to hear," Mr. Pottah said, and with a *click* the speaker turned off.

Cal swam through the ball pit to one side and climbed up a soft, furry ladder that wriggled under his hands. He was still a couple of stories underground.

Just past the ball pit room, he found a series of gears that turned on a two-story wall. They reminded him of the inside of a giant clock. As he stepped on the correct spinning gear, it would turn and lift him up to the next one. At the top of the gears, he found Butler in a long hallway filled with fake butterflies. The plastic insects swooped and dove around the dog, who tried to catch them in his mouth.

Cal led Butler out of the hallway, and they discovered Mrs. T. stuck in a wide pipe that spun around and around.

"I feel like I'm a penny in the dryer!" Mrs. T. said as she was tumbled about. Laughing, she managed to roll out of the spinning tube and wobbled to her feet next to Butler and Cal.

"Come on," Mrs. T. said. "I've been studying maps of the fun house online. I have a feeling I can guess where the others might have ended up."

Mr. T. and Bug were in the Autocorrect Room. When Cal, Mrs. T., and Butler walked in, Mr. T. was laughing so hard tears were rolling down his face.

"Say something else, Bug," Mr. T. wheezed between bursts of laughter.

"Trams m'I!" Bug announced in Bog.

A speaker in the wall asked, "Did you mean . . . ?"

and the walls of the room came to life. They showed pictures of aardvarks.

Butler barked, "Rabbo!" And the room asked, "Did you mean . . . ?"

Thousands of rabbits bounced along the walls.

Cal started laughing, too, but his stomach suddenly growled hungrily.

The room must have heard his belly, because it said, "Did you mean . . . ?"

And huge grizzly bears appeared on the walls.

"I think that growling means it's dinnertime!" Mrs. T. said. "Let's get Imo and grab something to eat."

Imo had never left the hall of mirrors. Rather than working her way out of the maze, she just started taking down the mirrored walls with her screwdriver.

"Hey!" Cal said. "That's cheating."

"You have fun your way," Imo said, "and I'll have it mine."

The family made their way outside, where the sun had set. A snack truck shaped like a covered wagon was parked in front of the fun house. Instead of pioneers, it was stuffed with brightly colored wrapped foods, chocolate candies, and salty, buttery treats.

"Enjoy it, guys," Mrs. T. told the family. "I'm going to

talk to the clowns about getting us something healthier to eat over the next five days."

As they ate on the steps of the fun house, Cal looked up at the sky. Back in Hawkins, they could see stars just about every night. Here, though, the stars were blocked by the blinking lights of the fun house.

"No stars tonight anyway, Cal," Mrs. T. said, guessing what he was thinking. "It's going to rain. Besides, if it felt just like we were home, it wouldn't be an adventure!"

"What do you say?" Mr. T. said when they had finished dinner. "Should we hit the hay?"

The Talaskas found bright-orange Funland sleeping bags and even brighter-orange Funland pajamas stacked near the entrance of the fun house. After changing into their pj's in the hall of mirrors, they found their way to a big, empty circular room with a raised round stage in the center. Mr. T. closed the door to keep out the honking, beeping, chirping, and flashing lights. Now it was nice and quiet inside.

"I'm not sure what this room does," Mrs. T. said. "I don't remember it on any of the maps online."

"It's just like camping," Cal said. The family dragged the sleeping bags up onto the round stage, and all of them crawled into their bags. Mr. T. took off his glasses, and Butler curled up at Bug's feet. They said good night, and as Cal was drifting off to sleep, he suddenly felt like he was spinning.

Must've eaten one too many corn dogs, he thought.

He opened his eyes and saw the crack of the door whiz by. A second later it went by again. And again. This time faster.

Either that was one powerful corn dog, or the room was actually spinning.

"Wake up!" Cal called out.

Imo shot straight up. "What? What is it?"

The whole room was spinning. Cal could feel the force tugging him toward the edge of the round stage. Mr. T. grabbed his glasses just before they slid off.

"Hold on!" Mrs. T. shouted, and then her pillow flew off the stage and hit the wall. The room was turning so fast that the pillow stayed stuck to the middle of the wall.

"We're in a centrifuge ride!" Imo shouted. "I have a feeling that as long as there's weight on this circle, the room won't stop spinning!"

With their legs and most of their bodies stuck in the sleeping bags, it was hard to hang on. Even though

Bug was desperately trying to hold on to Butler, the dog was the first one to get pulled off the stage. He skittered off the surface, sailed through the air, and landed on the padded wall on his side.

He barked, "Rabbo!" (which clearly meant *Hey, that wasn't so bad!*).

Moose went next, then Cal and Imo. Mrs. and Mr. T. flew off at the same time. All in their sleeping bags.

Bug was the last one on the stage, and he only let go so he could be closer to Butler. His little body sailed through the air, and Mrs. T. caught him.

Imo had been right. With no weight on the circle, the spinning stopped, and so did the force holding the family to the wall. They slid down to the floor, where they wriggled free of the sleeping bags.

Just in case the room started whirling again, the Talaskas stumbled dizzily out the door and gathered in the hall of mirrors.

"We need to find somewhere else to bunk down," Mrs. T. said. "We can't sleep outside, because it's raining."

Every room they tried in the fun house had a different problem that would keep them awake. Plastic ghosts popped up out of nowhere in one. Slimy robot bats flew over their heads in another. And everywhere they looked were clowns—stuffed clowns, giraffe clowns, floating clowns, swimming clowns—so many clowns!

Finally, the Talaskas were desperate just to put their heads down. They settled on a room shaped like a boat that swayed up and down from front to back as if it were riding the waves of a stormy ocean.

As they all lay down in the rocking room, Moose's eyes wobbled, and Cal felt his stomach getting queasy again. In fact, all of the Talaskas looked a little seasick—except for Mr. T. He stuck his hands in the air and played his invisible piano. His fingers kept making the same pattern over and over.

Cal laughed when he realized what he must be playing.

"Nice job with 'Row, Row, Row Your Boat,' Dad," he said, suddenly very tired.

As the room rocked him to sleep, Cal started dreaming about how tomorrow they would find the BLUE-PRINT and win this contest.

When they woke up in the morning, the Talaskas were a mess. Cal felt like he'd been thrown into a plastic bag and juggled by a giant clown all night.

"Rabbo?" Butler said sleepily, pawing at his eyes.

Mr. Pottah was waiting for them outside the fun house at the food wagon. He must have heard what Mrs. T. had said about all the junk food. The wagon now included fruit salad and yogurt. As the family ate breakfast, Cal noticed that while all the *bleeps*, *bongs*, and *bings* of the park's remaining rides were still in the air, the sounds of bulldozers and explosions were gone.

"Where are all the construction clowns?" Cal asked.

"Oh, they were sent off on . . . a special project," Mr. Pottah said. "Top-secret. Speaking of top-secret, are you ready for the clue about what you need to find in Fun-land in the next five days?"

"We know we have to find the BLUEPRINT," Imo said.

Mr. Pottah smiled. "Yes, that's true. But there's a second part of the clue that no one has ever revealed outside of this park. Do you all promise not to share this second part of the clue with anyone?"

"Yes," the Talaskas said at the same time, except for Bug, who said, "Sey," and Butler, who barked, "Rabbo."

"I don't suppose it matters who you tell, anyway," Mr. Pottah said more to himself than to them.

"Why?" Cal asked. "Because it's so hard?"

"Hmm, well . . ." The clown didn't really answer. Instead, he pulled out a slip of paper from his pocket. "So, here's the clue." He paused and read from the paper. "'Find the BLUEPRINT in the PALMTOPS!'"

Cal took the paper and reread the clue. Two of the words were written in all capital letters.

"This is the last you'll see of me," Mr. Pottah said.

Cal's thoughts flashed back to spinning into the wall in his sleeping bag. "What will we do if we get in trouble?" he asked.

"Don't worry," Mr. Pottah said. "You won't *see* me,

but we'll be watching you. Good luck!" And with that, he somersaulted away.

"That's it?" Cal said. "Find the BLUEPRINT in the PALMTOPS." He looked down at his hands and his own palms. "Palm tops? Is that what it means?" If he flipped his hands over, were those the tops of palms? Or were the tops of his palms his wrists? Or maybe his fingers?

"In my opinion, you're thinking way too small," Imo said, tugging her ear. "The BLUEPRINT isn't hidden on you; it's in the park somewhere."

Luckily, the Talaskas had an expert on their team. Cal asked, "Mom, where are there palm trees in Funland?"

"Over in Pharaoh's Kingdom," Mrs. T. said instantly. "And there used to be palm readers over in Haunted Land. But I don't think there are any people around."

"And that's not all," Mr. T. said. "In SportsWorld they *palm* basketballs."

"True," Mrs. T. said. "We've got our work cut out for us. The park is actually bigger than the whole town of Hawkins."

While they were the only visitors in the park today, Funland normally held an average of 52,000 visitors at any one time. It was huge. So finding a blueprint or any single object would be nearly impossible. That was why all the other families had failed. But if the Talaskas wanted to save their house, they had to be different.

They decided to start with Pharaoh's Kingdom. It seemed like the most obvious choice.

"Maybe we should split up and cover more ground?" Imo suggested.

"No," Cal said. "We're always better together. Let's go!"

"Walking to that part of the park will take at least forty-five minutes," Imo said. "Let's take a blimp! It'll be faster."

The blimps were like ski gondolas and used to carry visitors all over Funland. There were blimp stops in each section of the park. The Talaskas went to the nearest one and hopped on board. The blimp had windows on all sides, so it was like being inside a glass bubble.

As the blimp approached Pharaoh's Kingdom, the park's version of the Great Pyramid rose up into the air. A water ride called the Nile Adventure wrapped around the base of the pyramid and then spiraled away in crazy loops. The ride was surrounded by fake palm trees that were at least three stories high.

When they got off the blimp, a big red sign announced that the area would be demolished the following week because a fifty-six-year-old woman in Iowa didn't like it.

"What do we know about this pyramid, Mom?" Cal asked. He had to speak loudly enough to be heard over the rushing water of the nearby ride.

Mrs. T. tapped her head as if typing in search terms. "The real Great Pyramid is seven hundred fifty-six feet long on each side, four hundred eighty-one feet high, and composed of two point three million stones weighing an average of three tons each. This copy is about one-fifth the size of the real one."

"Does anyone see a blueprint anywhere?" Cal asked.

"Ekil kool?" Bug said to Butler. And Cal guessed he meant *What's a blueprint again?*

"Remember, it's a plan people use to build or redo something," Imo said. "It'll probably look like a rolled-up poster."

Mrs. T.'s eyebrows went up as she remembered something. "I'm going to be sorry I brought this up . . . ," she said. "But there's a theory that the five master builders of the Great Pyramid hid the blueprint for the pyramid at the top."

Mrs. T. went on to explain that there were five platforms at the point of the pyramid. Each of the four sides had a platform, and then there was a smaller one at the very top. When the five master builders stood on the platforms together, a compartment containing the blueprint opened up.

"Funland always chooses families with at least five people for the contest," Cal said. "Maybe there's a reason. Maybe it's because they need to stand on the platforms together and unlock a secret compartment!"

It sounded pretty nutty as Cal said it out loud, so he was surprised when Mr. T. said, "Okay, why not? Let's give it a shot!"

They gazed up over the water ride to the top of the pyramid. It was about four stories tall and a steep climb.

"What does this have to do with PALMTOPS?" Imo asked. And then answered her own question. "Maybe it's because we'll be able to see the tops of the palms from up there?"

Mrs. T. nodded. "Here's another question," she said. "How do we climb up the steep side of a pyramid?"

"I don't know," Cal said. "But even if one of us falls, we'll slide right into the water of the ride!"

Tugging her ear, Imo said, "Cal, you grab life jackets from the water ride. I'll take care of the climbing part." She trotted over to Pharaoh's Fairway, a mini-golf attraction, and came back with five golf putters. "We can use these like ice picks to climb."

After all the Talaskas had put on their life jackets, Imo studied the log flume that wrapped around the pyramid.

She found a narrow opening in one spot between the ride and the pyramid. She scooted up through the opening and stood on the lip of the water ride. She swung the putter over her head and connected with the fiberglass of the pyramid. The putter went through with a satisfying *thwick!*

"Imo!" Mrs. T. said automatically.

"It doesn't matter, Mom," Imo said. She pulled herself up along the putter's handle and braced her feet on the side of the pyramid. She looked like a mountain climber scaling Everest. Then she raised the putter and swung it again. "They're going to tear this down next week anyway!"

Cal climbed through the opening just behind Imo. He swung his putter into the pyramid. *Thwick!* He pulled himself up, got his balance, and kept going. After giving Butler instructions to stay put with Moose until they came down, Bug followed Mr. T. up the wall. Mrs. T. went behind him to catch him if he fell.

Cal wasn't sure if his mom would've been up for this climb even a couple of weeks ago. But she had been working on getting fitter. And she sped up the side at a fast pace.

Thwick! Thwick!

"Fore!" Cal cried, and brought the putter down again.

"For what?" Imo asked from up above.

"No, *fore!*" Cal said. "Oh, forget it." *Thwick!*

Five minutes later, they made it to the top. Just as

Mrs. T. had described, there were four platforms, one on each side of the pyramid, and one small platform at the top. The older Talaskas stood on the sides holding hands, and then Bug climbed to the very top.

This is the moment of truth, Cal thought.

Looking extremely tiny at the peak of such a huge structure, Bug planted his feet in the center, and . . .

Nothing happened. No secret compartment opened.

"Yllaer?" Bug said, which Cal figured must mean *Seriously?*

"Now . . . what . . . ?" Mrs. T. asked, red-faced and out of breath.

"You okay, honey?" Mr. T. asked her. Mrs. T. touched her headband, got a determined look on her face, and nodded.

"We can see the tops of every palm tree but one from up here," Cal said. "Anyone see a blueprint?"

They all scanned the fake trees. There wasn't anything. Cal was just about to give up when he noticed something. The water ride that wrapped around the pyramid also looped around the one tree whose top they couldn't see from up there.

"Check it out," Cal said. "Maybe the other families missed that tree! It might have the blueprint! We need to get to a spot over that tree. . . ."

"How are we going to do that?" Mrs. T. said. "Better question: How are we going to get back down?"

"The easy way," Cal said, and let go of his putter.

"Cal!" Mrs. T. shouted when she saw what he was thinking.

He grabbed hold of the putter again at the last fraction of a second. "Mom, it will be okay."

Mrs. T. looked down at the water below and seemed to think better of her reaction. "Actually, your idea sounds fun," she said. "Go for it!"

Cal let go again, and this time he slid on his rear end down the side of the structure. He wondered how many families in the history of the world could claim to be pyramid surfers. His mom probably knew the answer.

He hit the water of the flume ride and went under for a moment. Then the life jacket popped him to the surface. The current pushed him along at about twenty miles per hour.

"We have to stop in the middle of the tube!" he shouted back to his family. He should've mentioned this to them before.

Cal turned his body so that he was traveling legs first. He pushed his legs and his arms out to the side so they rubbed against the walls of the ride and acted like brakes. He stopped just a little above the spot where he wanted to be.

That was when Bug came shooting around the corner and barreled into him. Cal slid a few feet but managed not to get swept away.

"Bug and I are stopped here!" he shouted, but he had no idea if the rest of the family could hear him over the sound of running water.

Luckily, his dad had heard him. Mr. T. used the same technique Cal had used to slow down. He had Mrs. T.'s feet on one shoulder and Imo's on the other. They came to a stop right at the top of Cal's and Bug's heads.

Cal peered up over the edge of the flume ride—not easy with all the rushing water. He saw that they had been pushed too far down the ride. He couldn't quite see the top of the palm tree from this angle. He tried to get a little higher.

How is that going to happen? Cal wondered just as "Rabbo! Rabbo!" drifted down to them. It sounded like Butler was up at the start of the ride.

"Denetsil eh!" Bug said. Probably meaning *I told him not to move until we came back down from the pyramid. And, well, we came back down from the pyramid.*

"I just need to get a look at the top of that palm tree," Cal said.

He dragged himself back along his family's bodies so he could peer up over the edge.

"Rabbo?" Butler barked from above. The question in his voice made it sound like he was very tempted to come down the flume to join the family.

Cal knew there wasn't much time. When Butler came barreling around the corkscrew turn, he would knock into the rest of the family and send them flying.

Imo realized it, too. "Hurry, Cal!" she said. "What do you see?"

Holding on to Mr. T.'s arm, Cal pulled himself just a little higher. *All right!* Now he could see everything. He scanned the treetop. "There's—"

Wham! Forty-five pounds of wet dog slammed into the family at twenty miles an hour. The force was like a cork popping out of a bottle, and they shot down the water ride in a rolling ball of Talaska and hit the pool at the bottom with a giant splash.

"Cal, what were you going to say?" Imo sputtered. "Did you see the blueprint?"

Shaking water out of his ears, Cal said, "I was going

to say there's nothing. There wasn't any sign of a blue-print anywhere."

Cal decided not to panic . . . not yet, anyway. "Come on," he told his family. "Let's keep looking!"

14

Over the next four days, the Talaskas searched just about every inch of Funland.

Cal and Mr. T. rode Timmy Toadstool's Twists and Turns more times than Cal could count—and he worried it might give him bad dreams for the rest of his life. The ride was made for two-year-olds. But everyone else, including Bug, refused to go on it. The tiny cars were shaped like mushrooms, and the music playing during the ride sounded like a donkey kicking a xylophone while a shrieking chipmunk sang along.

Mr. T. and Cal jammed themselves into one of the mushroom cars, and the track jerked them through Timmy Toadstool's village. The dizzying twists and turns of the ride were so violent that Cal couldn't stay focused on one thing long enough to look for the blueprint.

"We have to go on it again, Dad," Cal said after the first time. "We need to make sure the blueprint isn't hidden somewhere on the ride."

"I don't know if I can," Mr. T. said, shaking his head like he wanted to knock the song loose. "But I can't think of another plan."

Mr. T. and Cal spent a total of six hours on the ride—and didn't find the blueprint.

On the same day, Bug, Butler, and Mrs. T. focused their search on the leaping fountains. These were streams of water that shot up out of the ground in time to perky music. Mrs. T. had an idea that they should stand on all the leaping fountains at once. She thought the pressure would unlock a secret compartment, just like in an ancient castle in Scotland she had read about. But they just ended up soaking wet and tired.

Imo didn't fare much better. She rode the Double Drop of Doom at least thirty-two times. She strapped herself into a seat and was dropped twenty stories on a bungee cord. A camera was timed to take a photo of the rider at the scariest moment. And this photo was sent to giant video screens all over the park. So pictures of Imo with her mouth wide open, her hair flying over her face, and her eyes bugging out were shown all day.

Cal wanted a vacation from this vacation. And the rest of the Talaskas felt the same way. They were tired of the honking horns, the blinking lights, the topsy-turvy floors, and the snack wagon food. They were ready for the old house on Piedmont Place, even if it was a wreck.

When they got up on the fourth morning, Mrs. T. mentioned that the "palm" in the clue could be a type of movie award. So they went to the movie theater and watched a biography about the Head Clown, Chad Lowen, twenty-two times. They looked for a clue in the movie, but there was nothing.

It had been another long day of running around the park, and the family was heading back to the fun house. As Moose trundled past him, Cal leaned against the Lamppost of Fun to catch his breath. Everywhere they went, Cal thought about BLUEPRINT and PALMTOPS. He couldn't shake the feeling that the answer was right in front of him.

The family only had one more day in the park. It was really getting down to the wire. Cal glanced up and saw Clown Castle on the hill, where Chad Lowen, founder of Funland and Head Clown, lived.

Maybe a visit to the Head Clown would help pick up their spirits.

When Cal suggested the idea to his family, they all shook their heads.

"But why not?" Cal said. "Mr. Pottah said we can go anywhere we want in Funland. And that nothing was off-limits. Come on. Who knows? The blueprint could be inside the castle. Plus, we'll meet clown royalty!"

"*Royal* palm is a kind of palm tree!" Imo said. "Maybe Cal's onto something; maybe the blueprint is in there."

They took a blimp over to Clown Castle and climbed the hill. The castle door was unlocked, and it opened with a single push. The family went inside. There was just one giant room, with a high-backed leather chair facing monitors that filled the far wall. Each screen showed what people around the world were saying about Funland.

The chair spun around.

It was Ms. Dowen.

"Oh, sorry, we were looking for—" Cal started to say, and then it all became clear in his head. "We're in the right place, aren't we?" he said. "We're actually looking for you."

Imo realized what he was saying. "You're the Head Clown, Ms. Dowen? You're Chad Lowen?"

". . . close the door, please . . . ," Ms. Dowen said, ". . . so the clowns can't get inside . . ."

Cal want to point out that this *was* Clown Castle, but he kept his mouth shut.

"My real name is Chadmina Lowen," the woman they had known as Ms. Dowen said. Now that the door was closed and there was no risk of riling up the clowns, she spoke at a normal volume. "My family called me Chad for short. I wore so much clown makeup back then, no one could tell if I was a woman or a man. So I just let people believe what they like."

"But Chad Lowen is the world's most famous clown!" Mrs. T. said. "You don't enjoy clowns at all."

"Some people didn't like me being a clown, so I stopped," Chad said. "And when I gave you my name that first time, you thought I said Dowen, and you seemed to like it."

"Oh," Mrs. T. said. "That's not good. You should be called whatever *you* want!"

Chadmina shook her head. "No, not in my business. What I *want* doesn't matter. It's what people *like* that's important!" She threw a hand toward the screens behind her. People's mean comments about Funland kept popping up. And Chadmina was clearly having a tough time not looking at them. Finally, she gave up and turned back toward the screens.

Cal thought about all the times Chadmina had been glued to her phone. She must have been reading people's comments and responding. She was desperate to have everyone like everything she did.

"That's why the park renovations are taking so long,"

Imo said, thinking the same thing as Cal. "You're so worried about what each person likes."

"Of course!" Chadmina said, as if that should be the most obvious thing in the world. "See for yourself. It's crushing." She pointed to a screen in front of her. Cal had to lean in to see what she was talking about. A single thumb pointing down.

"You mean this one?" Cal asked. "There's only one person in England who didn't like the idea for a drinking fountain next to the Double Drop of Doom. And he didn't even say why."

Chad shuddered again. "It's the silent insults that sting the most," she said. "That's why I'm tearing down that ride."

Cal laughed, thinking that she was back to being a clown and making a joke. But her face was serious.

"You can't keep bulldozing things each time someone says something negative," Imo said. "Some people can be pretty horrible online." She touched one of her hair clips. Cal realized that Imo must have seen the mean online comment about her and her clips after all.

"I'd say ninety-nine percent of the people don't even really mean what they're saying," Mrs. T. said. "Sometimes you just have to go with your gut instinct."

"You can't take online stuff so seriously," Mr. T. said. "What you've built in this park is amazing—really!"

Chadmina shook her head. All their encouragement was lost on her.

"We can prove it to you," Cal said. "Can you give me a printout of some of the things people say, please?"

"Why not?" Chadmina said miserably. She printed out six pages of comments for them. Without really knowing what else to say, the Talaskas wished Chadmina a good night and left her staring at her screens.

Back in the fun house, Cal's family tried to ask him what he was up to with the printouts, but Cal didn't answer them until the next morning when they were eating breakfast.

"I have a plan," he said. "You know how ideas come to you when you're thinking about something else?"

Imo nodded. "I think I know what you mean. We've been so worried about finding the blueprint that our brains are worn out. We need to give them a break."

"Dad, I think you should write a song using these comments as lyrics," Cal said. "And, Mom, you can add trivia stuff you know about the park."

"I don't think I get it," Mrs. T. said.

"It will help us brainstorm about the blueprint," Cal

said. "And more important, it will show that the cruel comments people make shouldn't matter at all."

"Good idea, Cal," Mrs. T. said. "Give us a couple of minutes and we can come up with something."

Chadmina had been right about one thing. There were some pretty horrible things posted by users on the Funland site. But with his glasses on a slant, Mr. T. set them to music and wrote one of the catchiest songs Cal had ever heard. Mr. T. sprinkled the mean comments with fun trivia facts about the park that Mrs. T. had found online.

The whole family gathered around the picnic table once the song was finished. As Mr. T. played an invisible keyboard on the table, the family sang,

"What don't I not like? What don't I not like at Funland?
Can it be the foul forty-foot-high Fungus Hill?
Or the sick frond forts found over in StarVille?
Just take a gander at the bland blueprint of fun
And you'll see why it's forever my number one!
Then turn your gaze to the left or to the right,
Or backward or forward to find not even a mite
That I don't not like, I don't not like at Funland!"

"Stop!" Imo shouted.

"What?" Cal said. "We're not that bad."

Imo shook her head. "I hate to admit it, Cal, but I think you were right. This song might've just unlocked the answer to where the blueprint is hidden!"

"What do you mean?" Cal asked.

"A frond is a leaf on a palm tree," Imo said. "The roofs over in StarVille are made of palm fronds! The blueprint could be there on *top* of the palm leaf roofs!" Imo jumped up from the table.

"Wait, honey," Mrs. T. said. "We'll go with you after Bug's done eating."

"It's no big deal," Imo said. "I'll just ride a blimp over. I'll be right back. Okay?"

Mr. and Mrs. T. agreed. They watched as Imo hustled to the blimp station to hop into a glass bubble. While they waited for Imo to come back, the family decided they might as well give the song another try.

When they got to the line about "the bland blueprint of fun," Cal said, "Sing it in all capital letters, Dad. I can tell you're not." He was trying to make a joke, but something serious hit him.

He slapped his hand over his mouth. "Of course! All caps! BLUEPRINT should be in all caps!"

"Os?" Bug asked.

"BLUEPRINT is an anagram!" Cal said.

"What?" Mr. T. said.

"That's why the clowns went crazy every time we called Butler's name!" Cal said. "The secret is an anagram." When they still didn't catch on, he said, "Rearrange the letters for BLUEPRINT so that *butler* is one of the words."

Mr. T. scribbled the words on the sheet in front of him. "You get *butler pin!*"

"The pin!" Mrs. T. said. "The one that fell off the Lamppost of Fun—"

"Holy Aristotle!" Cal realized something else. "PALMTOPS is another anagram. It stands for *lamppost*! The clue says, 'You'll find the butler pin on the lamppost!'"

"Where is the pin now?" Mrs. T. asked.

"It's stuck on Moose, remember?" Cal said. "It got jammed in his Like slot."

They looked down at their feet. Moose had been right there, but now he was gone.

"That song!" Cal said. "Moose heard Imo singing *left, right, forward,* and *backward.* He followed her voice commands. I don't know how many times we sang that song. He could be headed anywhere in the park by now!"

They ran toward the blimp. Imo was just leaving the station, rising up the wire that would carry her across the park. There was no way to stop the blimp or turn it around. Cal jumped and waved to get her attention. She turned and looked at them from inside the glass bubble.

"BLUEPRINT is an anagram!" Cal shouted.

She slapped her forehead. *Oh, of course!* They couldn't hear her through the glass, but they could read her lips. *Butler pin!*

Then her eyes went automatically to find Moose. Her mouth formed a *No!* She pointed behind them. From her high spot, she could see things they couldn't see from the ground. *There he is!* she shouted silently. *You have to stop him!*

Imo pressed her hands against the glass like she was trying to yell through it. *Moose doesn't just listen to me!* she said. *He'll also listen to—*

And then the blimp carried her out of view.

The rest of the Talaskas ran in the direction where Imo had pointed.

Mrs. T. was out of breath, and Mr. T. stopped with

her. "You guys go ahead and grab Moose," Mr. T. said to Bug, Butler, and Cal. "We'll catch up with you in a second."

Cal nodded and took off running again with Bug and Butler.

"On ho!" Bug shouted. And Cal could see why. The sun glittered off Moose's antlers as he trundled into a construction zone up ahead. What had once been the Double Drop of Doom ride was now just a pit twenty stories deep. Moose rolled underneath the protective fence and out on a steel beam that jutted over the hole.

Cal stopped Bug and Butler at the fence. It wasn't safe for them to go any farther.

In seconds, Moose would roll off the beam and into the pit. The Talaskas would never be able to get him back out, and the butler pin would be gone.

"Moose, stop!" Cal shouted. He knew he wasn't the one Moose would listen to, but he had to try.

Imo had told them that Moose was programmed to listen to just two people. But everyone in the family had tried talking to Moose.

Everyone but one person, Cal realized. He looked at his little brother and Butler. "It's you."

Butler barked. "Rabbo?"

"No, not you, Butler," Cal said. "The other person who can talk to Moose is you, Bug."

Bug squinted up at Cal like he was nuts. But he opened his mouth and made a few gibberish sounds. Moose kept rolling along. He was just a couple of feet from the end of the steel beam.

"Not like that, Bug," Cal said, trying to keep calm. "You have to talk like you would to one of us."

Bug looked at Butler, whose tail twirled in a way that said *Go ahead*. Bug took a deep breath and said:

"MOOSE, STOP! MOOSE, ROLL BACKWARD!"

A split second went by, and then Moose's eyes woggled. He stopped and rolled toward them. A few moments later, he wheeled back under the fence.

"Stop!" Bug said, and Moose came to a halt at their feet.

Cal gave his brother a high five. "Outstanding, Bug. Way to go!"

Just then, their parents and Imo joined them. Everyone was out of breath but smiling from ear to ear. "You did it!" Imo said. The Talaskas went in for a giant group hug, and Butler got up on his hind legs to join in.

"We won the makeover!" Cal shouted. "They're going to fix up our house on Piedmont Place!"

"*Going* to? Oh no," Mr. Pottah said. His voice came from a speaker on top of a nearby hot-dog stand. "No, no, not *going* to."

The Talaskas stopped jumping up and down. They turned toward the speaker. "What do you mean?" Cal asked in shock. "We did it!"

"How can you do something when it's already—" Mr. Pottah started to say, and then interrupted himself. "I don't want to give away the surprise."

"You have to live up to your end of the agreement," Imo said. "It's only fair!"

"We saw that you won the contest within five minutes of being in Funland," Mr. Pottah said. "You Talaskas really are natural contest winners. You can't NOT win. Amazing. But we didn't want the fun to end there!"

The fun? Cal thought. He was starting to realize that maybe he and his family had a different definition of fun than the Clown Patrol did.

"We'll take you back to your home in the morning," Mr. Pottah said. "We need time to set up the camera crew there to show just how much you LIKE everything! In the meantime, have a fun night!"

Cal felt like a sponge that had soaked up too much water . . . or too much fun. He wouldn't mind not hearing that three-letter word for a while.

al didn't think he could take another night in the fun house. He wanted to leave. Right this second. The rest of the Talaskas didn't need any convincing.

"What about our luggage?" Imo asked.

"We'll call from home and ask the clowns to bring everything when they come to film us tomorrow," Mrs. T. replied. "Let's go."

"Hold on," Cal said. "We need to get the keys to the Flying Monkey."

They all looked up at the T. rex that loomed over the waterfall next to the fun house. As always, the twenty-foot-tall dinosaur was frozen in a battle with the hulking brontosaurus.

"Mr. Pottah said the timer on the T. rex's mouth

won't unlock until tomorrow," Imo reminded them. "And the car keys are inside."

Cal and Imo went to stand behind the panels that controlled the movement of the dinos. Running her eyes over the buttons and switches, Imo said, "There's no way to unlock the T. rex's mouth early. We'll have to wait."

Cal groaned. He couldn't take it. They were so close to going home, and now this! Frustrated, he wiggled one of the joysticks on the panel. The T. rex's front claw jabbed into the brontosaurus.

Without hesitating, Imo pushed the joystick in front of her, and the bronto jabbed the T. rex back.

Suddenly it was as if Cal and Imo were in the backseat on a long car ride, getting on each other's nerves.

"Don't do that!" Cal said, and flicked the T. rex's tail so it whapped into the bronto's leg.

Annoyed, Imo gave three pokes back to the T. rex. "Knock. It. Off!"

The sharp movements made the T. rex's jaw wiggle, and his mouth opened slightly. Cal could see the glint of the car keys between its fangs.

"Careful, kids," Mrs. T. warned. "Let's not break anything else!"

"It's working, Mom," Cal said. "If we keep at it, we might jostle the keys loose!"

Mrs. T. nodded, so Cal and Imo continued poking and jabbing with the dinos. To help out, Bug and Butler stepped in front of the control panels.

"Watch us!" Bug said, and he and Butler started wrestling. Mostly it was just the two of them wiggling and jiggling on the ground. Imo and Cal copied their wacky moves with the dinosaurs. Finally, all the jerking back and forth and up and down shook the keys loose. They fell from the T. rex's mouth and splashed into the pool at the bottom of the dino waterfall.

In a flash, Mr. T. waded into the shallow water.

"You'll get drenched, Dad!" Imo called.

"I'm happy to get wet-toed if it means we can hit the road!" The water went up to Mr. T.'s knees, and he reached down. When his hand came back up, he was holding the car keys. "Got them!"

The family headed straight for the parking lot. They tried to stay out of the bright lights and stick to the shadows as they made their way down SuperFun Street.

"Escape from Funland!" Bug said, and scratched Butler behind the ears.

Mrs. T. held a finger to her lips. "Shh," she whispered. "It's not really an escape. . . ."

Cal laughed. "Then why are you whispering, Mom?"

In an imitation that would have made James proud, Mrs. T. said, like Ms. Dowen, ". . . just don't want to rile up the clowns . . ."

Mr. T. chuckled and then slapped a hand over his mouth to stay quiet. They snuck out the front gates. Cal was pretty sure that hidden cameras must be watching them.

But who cared? They had won the contest and they were going home!

As they pulled out of the parking lot, Cal couldn't wait to get back to Piedmont Place. And he wasn't alone. Bug didn't ask to stop at a single rest area the whole way.

Imo asked Mrs. T. to reach into the glove compartment for her favorite pair of pliers.

Cal said, "Imo, why did you program Moose so that he would listen to Bug?"

Using the pliers to carefully pry the butler pin out of Moose, Imo explained that she had wanted to show Bug something. Just as Butler and Bug shared their own language, Imo and Moose shared their own, too. But she still talked with other people. It was Imo's way of showing Bug that he could have a bond with someone special *and* still connect with other friends and family.

"Wow." Cal whistled. "Impressive."

"Way to go, honey," Mrs. T. said from the front seat. "What do you have to say for yourself, Bug?"

"I want to go home." Bug leaned over and gave Butler a hug around the neck. Butler's tail beat a quick rhythm against the seat.

An hour later, Imo had freed the butler pin and handed it to Cal. He wrapped his fingers around it. He couldn't believe this little pin was going to change their lives in such a big way. Finding it meant they would be able to live in their house forever.

Two hours after leaving Funland, the Talaskas were on the outskirts of Hawkins. They drove past Mr. Palmer's farm and the giant billboard he rented out to the Wish Shoppe. They turned off Main Street onto Piedmont Place, and Cal felt his heart skip a beat. The whole family was looking out the front window, trying to get the first glimpse of their favorite place on the planet.

Their house.

When they pulled up to the front, Cal had that feeling that Bug and Butler must have when they haven't seen each other for even a few minutes. He wanted to roll and squirm happily on the grass.

But there wasn't any grass.

Instead there were plastic flowers that kind of

waved and bobbed in the setting sun. "Hello!" and "Good evening!" a few chirped. Others didn't seem to be working correctly. They just shouted, "Blah!"

The flowers were a little scary.

"Where did these come from?" Cal asked. "And who closed all the curtains in the house?"

No one had answers. Cal's eyes went to the driveway. In their excitement about getting home, they had all missed seeing that another car was already parked there, closer to the garage. "Whose minivan is that?" Imo asked, squinting at the license plate.

Cal did the same. The minivan was from Illinois, and the license plate read WR BNTNS. "That's a strange plate," Cal said.

Mr. T. was wiping his glasses on his shirt, so he couldn't make out the minivan. "What's it say?"

Cal tried sounding the letters out. Not easy with the flowers chattering away. "W . . . R . . . We are . . . B-N-T . . . Bent . . . N-S . . . We are Bentons!"

"The Bentons?" Imo said. "Why does that name sound familiar?"

"Oh no." Mr. T. looked stunned as he adjusted his glasses and read the license plate for himself. "I know."

Mrs. T. seemed just as worried. "The Bentons are

the family from Chicago who want to buy the house! We told them they could stay overnight here whenever they wanted!"

"Uh-oh," Bug said.

"We never called them to tell them we wouldn't be here," Mrs. T. said. "Or that the deal was off."

"You mean the Bentons are still going to buy the house?" Cal asked.

"Oh no," Mr. T. repeated. "I'm so . . ." And he couldn't finish. But Cal knew what he was thinking. *I'm so sad that we're going to lose the house after all.*

"Now that the Bentons are here, I'm worried it's too late," Mrs. T. said.

"Well, we might as well go inside and say hello," Mr. T. said.

And goodbye, Cal thought.

They all trudged miserably up the walk and opened the front door . . .

. . . and found themselves looking at a hall of mirrors.

"Funland?" Bug asked, shocked, and Butler barked, "Rabbo!"

"Come on," Cal said, and led the way through the maze of mirrors. The path was just the same as it was in the Funland Fun House. Beyond the hall of mirrors, the staircase was now a series of shifting steps, and next to that was a giant spinning tube. Through the back window, Cal could see that Imo's workshop was now a Clown Lounge.

How did Cal know? Because a big neon sign blinked out the words CLOWN LOUNGE.

"The clowns did this," Mrs. T. said. "They started working on the house the second we found the pin.

They've had five days to turn our house into a fun house!"

What might once have made Cal the happiest kid on the planet now made him one of the most freaked out.

The house was a tiny replica of the Funland Fun House.

"Hello, Bentons!" Mr. T. called out.

But there was no answer.

"Okay, we need to find that family!" Mrs. T. said.

The Talaskas had lived in a fun house for almost five days. They were pros when it came to figuring out how to get around without falling through a trapdoor, getting stuck on a wall, or being launched into the air. But not the Bentons.

The kitchen had been transformed into a centrifuge—just like the room where the Talaskas had tried to sleep.

The old floor, including the board that squeaked "Hi," had been torn up and replaced with padding.

"Oh no," Mrs. T. said as she walked across the new floor.

"The Bentons might have gone upstairs to go to sleep," Imo said.

The Talaskas made their way up the back stairs to the second floor. There, everything beeped and blinked just as in the original Funland Fun House. Cal opened the door to his and Bug's bedroom, and it seemed the same as when they'd left. Mr. T. went in first and walked toward Cal's bed.

"Don't move, Dad!" Cal said, and Mr. T. froze. "There's a trapdoor right in front of your feet."

Mr. T. looked down. "You're right."

Over the sounds of beeping and honking, Cal thought he could hear something. Butler cocked his head to the left. He must have been hearing it, too. He inched up to the trapdoor, sniffed the edges, and let out a very tiny "Rabbo . . . ?"

Cal crouched down to listen and then he heard it, too. Someone was calling "Help!"

"Oh man," Cal said. "I think the Bentons are down there."

"Down where?" Imo said. "We don't even know where it goes!"

"One way to find out," Cal said. He stepped on the trapdoor and it dropped open.

A slide—like the one Cal had always wanted in his room—carried him toward the basement.

It shot straight down two stories and was more of a hole than a slide. Luckily, the basement had been transformed into a giant bouncy room. The four Bentons and their cat were all there, struggling to get off the springy surface without falling over. They were flopping around when Cal fired out of the slide and landed next to them.

"Hi," Cal said to the Bentons as they jiggled up and down. "I'm Cal Talaska."

"What kind of house is *this*?" asked the man who Cal supposed must be Mr. Benton. He gave new meaning to the term *completely wigged out*. His hair was standing straight up. "We wanted to film a reality show here. There's nothing *real* about this place!"

"It's about to get a little more crowded down here," Cal said. "We might want to move out of the way."

Seconds later, the rest of the Talaskas shot down onto the soft pad. Everyone bounced around like Ping-Pong balls—except Butler, who managed to touch down on all fours.

"Why, hello, Bentons!" Mrs. T. said once they had all stopped ricocheting off each other.

The Bentons didn't respond. They looked terrified.

"There is no way we're going to buy this house," Mrs. Benton said.

"Let's all calm down," Mr. T. said. "We can show you around—"

"We're getting out of here!" Mr. Benton said. "Or we'd like to!"

"There should be a staircase right over there," Cal said. The Bentons followed him up the stairs. They panicked again when they saw the hall of mirrors. Cal led the family through the maze and opened the front door. Bright light like the sun suddenly shone on them.

Cal held up his hand to shield his eyes, and then he saw that the light came from ten different video cameras held by the Funland Clown Patrol. Chadmina Lowen and Mr. Pottah were with them.

"Hello, Talaskas!" Mr. Pottah shouted. "Please tell our live global audience what you think of your new fun house?"

Just then the Bentons pushed past Cal to get out the front door, screaming at the top of their lungs. The cameras swung around to follow the Bentons racing toward their car like they were being chased by a pack of werewolves. Still screaming, they piled into their minivan and squealed out of the driveway. The van sped down Piedmont Place and out of sight.

For a moment, not even the clowns could lighten the mood.

Chadmina took a step forward. She clicked off all the bright lights of the cameras and then glared at the Talaskas' feet. ". . . that just went out live to millions of viewers . . . imagine the comments I'll get now . . ."

"Sorry about that," Cal said. And the other Talaskas mumbled apologies, too.

". . . you left Funland early . . . you went into the house without our cameras . . . the deal is off . . ."

"You have to fix our house!" Mrs. T. said.

". . . we did . . . and you broke the rules . . . we gave you a fun house, but your town will not get ten thousand dollars . . . goodbye . . ."

With that, Chadmina herded the Clown Patrol to the street. It took a few long minutes for them to pack into the clown car, and then it took off just as quickly as the Bentons had.

The Talaskas were left standing in the middle of the plastic talking flowers. "Nighty-night!" and "Blah! Blah!" the flowers chattered.

"Now what?" Mr. T. said. "Do you want to go back into the house?"

Everyone looked at each other with an expression that said the same thing: *No way.*

"We can't sleep here," Mrs. T. said.

The blinking lights and the sound effects would keep them awake all night, just as they had done at Funland.

"It's too late to wake up the neighbors . . . ," Imo said.

". . . and they're probably not too happy with us right now anyway," Cal added.

They piled into the Flying Monkey and headed over to Grandma Gigi's. After she let them in, they explained what had happened. Her eyes flashed when she heard about Chadmina breaking their deal. But she didn't ask any questions. She just pointed them to the guest room, which had two double beds.

Mr. and Mrs. T. took one. And Imo, Bug, and Cal took the other. Butler piled into the middle, snuggling up next to Bug.

Normally, Butler's dog breath and his sleep-barking with Bug would have kept Cal up. But it had been such a crazy week that he went right to sleep.

When the Talaskas woke up early the next morning, Gigi was gone.

She had left them a note on the kitchen counter with just one word: HOUSE.

The Flying Monkey turned to pull into the driveway of 914 Piedmont Place, but there wasn't any
room. Cars and trucks filled the driveway and were
parked all along the street.

"Oh no, now what are the clowns doing?" Mr. T. said.
"Who knows what they might have brewing?"

They climbed out of the car to find out what else
had been changed on the inside of their poor house.
As they shuffled up the front walk, they saw that the
plastic flowers were still there, but they had stopped
shouting.

"Maybe they're sleeping?" Bug asked. To Cal,
hearing Bug speak was still more startling than the
talking flowers.

The sounds of hammering and the buzzing of electric saws filled the air.

"No, no more fun," Cal said, and Imo nodded.

"In my opinion," she said, "I don't think we can *take* much more fun."

As if they were entering a haunted house, the Talaskas walked slowly up the steps to the front door. It swung open just as they got there.

Grandma Gigi stood in the doorway. Her bright eyes flashed at them. "Hi, Nelson and Maggie," she said to Mr. and Mrs. T. And then to the kids and Butler, "Hi there, grandpups."

"You're here!" Bug said in surprise.

Gigi raised an eyebrow. "Did you get that detailed note I left?" she said with a wink. That was her sign that she was making a joke.

"What are all those cars and trucks doing out here?" Mrs. T. asked nervously. "Is the house filled with clowns?"

"Hmm," Gigi said. "That's a matter of opinion. Why don't you come inside and see for yourself."

She opened the door wider and stepped aside. The family went into their house. Cal prepped himself for the hall of mirrors and the blinking lights and the shift-ing floors.

But that wasn't what he found.

As the Talaskas got an eyeful of their front hall, Mrs. T.'s hand went to her mouth and she gasped.

There weren't any mirrors; there weren't any clowns bouncing around or performing tricks. There were just regular people, people Cal had known his whole life, and they were everywhere.

James and his dad passed through the front hall carrying what looked like the old kitchen cabinets.

"Hey, Captain!" James said. "Welcome home!" Gigi gave him a stern look that said *Keep working*, and he just grinned. "Got to get this to the kitchen. See you in a minute."

Ms. Graves was on the stairs. She had plastic safety goggles on and was prying up the shifting steps so they could be replaced with a regular staircase. Leslie was on the step below her, using a crowbar with Alison. They both wore safety goggles, too.

Cal couldn't stop gaping at the sight of Leslie helping them. She caught his astonished look.

"See?" Leslie said. "I *am* the world's best friend. What? It's not—"

"I guess it's not bragging," Cal interrupted, and pointed at her eyewear, "if you can *goggle* it."

"Ugh," Leslie said. "Don't kill the moment, Cal." She and Alison got back to work.

And there were so many others working. Constance MacGuire from across the street and all her kids were hanging the Talaskas' old door leading to the living room. The Swaney twins were taking up the glowing tiles. The Rivales were standing in a pyramid, helping to rehang the chandelier.

The whole town was there. Mr. T. took Mrs. T.'s hand. They both had tears in their eyes.

"Why?" Imo said.

"Why what?" Gigi asked her.

Cal knew what Imo meant. "The clowns from Funland made it look like we were being so mean to everyone the day we left," he said. "I thought they would be mad at us. You know, not Like us."

"All that online Like business is nonsense," Grandma Gigi said. "This is how it looks when people really *like* you."

Cal knew she was right.

Gigi's eyes turned to Mr. and Mrs. T. "Once I made a few calls and let them know you needed help, the volunteers poured in," she said. "I hope you don't mind that I oversaw the changes you were looking for. The plumbing, the wiring, the stairs, those sorts of things."

"Oh no," Mrs. T. said, and reached a hand toward Gigi.

"I realize change is necessary, dear," Gigi said. She took Mrs. T. by the arm and led her into the kitchen. The rest of the family wandered after them in a daze.

"Yes, change is necessary," Gigi repeated. "But I did ask the volunteers to put a few things back just as they were."

"What do you mean?" Mrs. T. asked as she walked toward the counter. "I don't see—"

"Hi!" the floor under Mrs. T.'s foot squeaked.

"Oh!" Mrs. T. said. "The squeak is back!"

"Do you like it?" Gigi asked.

"I love it," Mrs. T. said. And now she didn't hesitate. She gave Gigi the biggest hug Cal had ever seen.

"I've got to get in on all this building!" Imo said. "I'm going to grab my extra tool belt."

After she was gone, Gigi said, "Imo is going to love what they did to her workshop."

Then Gigi opened the garage door. "You never park the Flying Monkey in the garage, do you?" She didn't wait for an answer. "That's good. Because it's now Bug and Butler's Stunt Room."

From floor to ceiling, the garage was covered in thick, rubbery padding. The two of them could play there, dream up whatever wacky stunts they wanted to fake, and they'd be totally safe.

Cal's parents, Bug, and Butler rushed inside. But Gigi stopped Cal.

"We didn't get rid of quite everything the clowns put in," she said, and waggled a finger for him to follow her up the back stairs.

She showed him the room where she stayed during visits. A small merry-go-round spun inside, just like the one she had drawn on the back of the Like sheet.

"Now for your room, Cal." Gigi led the way. Once they were there, she pointed at the floor where the trapdoor had been. There was still a hatchway, but now it had a lock on it. "Maybe you can guess the combination of the lock?" she asked with a wink.

Cal spun the dial on the lock until the combination read GRANDPUP, and it released with a click. He opened the hatchway, and the slide he had always wanted was still intact. It ran two stories down to his Contest Incubator in the basement.

"Thanks, Grandma G," Cal said, and hugged her.

"Only the best for my favorite grandpup," Gigi said. Then she stood up straight. "All right, enough nonsense. We have work to do!"

And work they did. For the next six hours, the Talaskas and the hundreds of volunteers transformed the fun house back into *their* house. Ms. Donegan came by with her food truck and fed the whole crew. Everyone took a break, sprawling on the front lawn next to the now-silent flowers.

Grilled chicken, beans, and potatoes . . . followed by

apple pie. Sitting next to James, Cal felt it was the first real meal he'd had in five days.

"Thanks, Ms. Donegan!" James said when he was finished.

Ms. Donegan chuckled as she wiped her hands on her apron. "James, you can call me Janey. We're almost family now."

"Um . . . ," James said, clearly not sure if he was going to be able to pull that off. He turned to Cal. "Guess what?" he said. "My dad and Ms. Donegan are getting married."

Cal wasn't sure this day could get any better. After lunch, he grabbed a paintbrush and started helping Mr. and Mrs. T. paint the patio. As they worked happily, something nagged at him. And then he realized what it was.

"What about the ten thousand dollars the town was going to get?" Cal asked. "Do they know they're not getting it?"

Mrs. T. laughed, and Mr. T. started humming the tune of the Funland song the family had written together the day before. Cal figured it was because he was nervous about telling the town they weren't going to get the money after all.

"Dad, it's okay . . . ," Cal said.

"No, that's not nerves, that's the sound of money." Mr. T. put down his paintbrush and reached into his pocket. He took out a check with the Talaskas' name on it. "We might not have won this contest, but I did sell that song for ten thousand dollars. And we'll give it to the town."

"That's amazing," Cal said. "But who bought it?"

Mr. T. nodded over at the corner of the yard. Chadmina Lowen was standing there in the shade of a tree, looking down at her phone. "She said she came to bring us our luggage," Mr. T. said. "She wants to use our song for the new theme music for Funland when they reopen . . . in a few years."

"I have something I want to give her," Cal said. After they were done with the patio, he wandered over to Chadmina.

She didn't look up, but Cal held out the butler pin. She stopped swiping. And for a second she didn't move. Then she put her phone in her pocket and took the pin, attaching it to her shirt.

It was like watching his mom put on her sweatband.

Once she had the pin on, Chadmina straightened and lifted her face. For the first time, Cal saw her eyes.

They were bright blue. "Thank you," she said. And now that her head was up, she seemed to notice where she was for the first time. "I'm sorry about your house."

"That's okay," Cal said. "You want to help fix it?"

"No, *Like* it or not, those were the rules," Chadmina said with a wink. "Besides, I think you and your friends have things under control." Her gaze fell on a group of workers. They were carefully chiseling the freshly dried concrete near the sliding glass door. "But you should tell them not to put back the cracks in the patio."

"Why?" Cal asked. "The cracks will make a smiling face if you look at it right."

Chadmina shook her head. "I saw the ad your parents put online to sell the house. One person commented that they didn't like it."

Cal remembered that mean post. "Sure. But we're the ones who live here. And we like it. Or at least I do."

"I do, too," Chadmina said. And then she added, "You know, there are a lot of things I like."

Something about her voice and the way her eyes lit up told Cal she was talking about Funland.

He could see Chadmina's lips twitch as she watched the smile being chiseled into the patio. It was as if her own smile were trying to crack through as well.

"Maybe I'll reopen the park in a few months," she finally said. "Maybe even in a couple of weeks." Nodding, she started walking toward the side of the house. "See you later, Cal."

"Wait, my family will want to say goodbye!" Cal called after her.

"I'll be out front picking flowers," Chadmina said without turning around. "And trying to make a person or two laugh. We'll see."

Cal stood for a second just enjoying being home. In his backyard, at his house. With all of his friends. Over the sounds of hammering and sawing, he swore he heard a bell ringing.

"I think you know what to do, Cal," Gigi called from the garage door. "I'll leave you to it. I have people to boss around."

The ringing sound was getting louder as Cal rushed inside and up the back stairs to his room. He spun the combination lock on the hatch in the floor. He lifted the door and jumped down the slide.

"Hoolllyyy Arisstotle!" he shouted as he flew down two stories and landed in the mini ball pit in the basement. He looked up. There were his parents, Bug, Butler, and Imo, who was ringing the family bell. They were standing next to Cal's Contest Incubator, the box filled with his greatest contest ideas.

Cal let out another whoop. The box hadn't been thrown away!

With one smooth move, Mr. T. plucked Cal out of the ball pit and set him next to the family so they all stood in a huddle.

"Okay, Cal," Mrs. T. said with a grin. "What's next for the Prizewinners of Piedmont Place?"